Advance praise for *T*

"A subtly musical voice, untrammeled storytelling, beyond the beaten paths of folklore and picturesque charm that we associate with Arab literature or, to be more exact, what we imagine to be Arab literature, and at the same time, with a stroke of genius—and this is the most delightful and important thing—that knows how to pay tribute to those same beaten paths by following them all the way to their source, deepening and adding perspective to a millennial Arab culture."
— **Ersi Sotiropoulos**

"Mansoura Ez-Eldin's novel has the brilliance and mystery of a marvelous gem."
— **Damien Aubel, *Transfuge***

"In this captivating and remarkably translated novel, Mansoura Ez-Eldin invites us to a round trip in time and space, between Cairo and Basra in Iraq, to meet timeless characters in a story which subtly mixes fiction and historical reality."
— **Nadia Leila Aissaoui, *L'Orient le Jour***

"A polyphonic story where she brilliantly combines the codes of ancient Arabic writing and those of the contemporary novel ... [A] labyrinthine narration where we get lost, like in the alleys of an Arab medina, with delight."
— **Richard Jacquemond, *Le Monde des Livres***

THE
ORCHARDS
OF BASRA

BY MANSOURA EZ-ELDIN
TRANSLATED BY PAUL G. STARKEY

I

Interlink Books

An imprint of Interlink Publishing Group, Inc.
Northampton, Massachusetts

First published in 2025 by

Interlink Books
An imprint of Interlink Publishing Group, Inc.
46 Crosby Street, Northampton, MA 01060
www.interlinkbooks.com

Originally published in Arabic in 2020 as *Basatin al-Basra*,
Dar al-Shorouq, Cairo

Library of Congress Cataloging-in-Publication data available
ISBN-13: 978-1-62371-621-9

Printed and bound in the United States of America

"As for jasmine, it was related that a man came to al-Hasan al-Basri, may God have mercy on him, and said: 'Yesterday I had a vision of angels descending from the heavens to pick jasmine from Basra.' Al-Hasan delved into his memory and said: 'That means the disappearance of the Basra ulema.' It is said that jasmine indicates trouble and sadness, because the first syllable of its name in Arabic means despair."

—*The Great Interpretation of Dreams* attributed to Muhammad Ibn Sirin

"Dreams are a decrepit narrative, consisting of the ruins of memory."

—Roland Barthes, *The Rustle of Language*, translated by Richard Howard

A TURQUOISE SKY WORTHY OF A PRECIOUS STONE

1

Yesterday I ate a moon.

I remember a street on which a few people were scattered, like extras in a silent film in which I was the only hero, spying on them through a chink in a wall separating me from life. I remember raising my head toward the sky and seeing a double moon, or to be more precise, a moon with its own reflection visible beside it, the two clinging together as if there was a hidden mirror joining them.

Afterward, I noticed two other reflections of the pair, one on the right and the other on the left. I was surprised that my sky should have six moons in it, or rather, three pairs of moons, but it was a cautious surprise, like opening the door to our apartment and finding a black cat waiting on the stairs.

I didn't notice until later that my sky the previous night was colored with a touch of turquoise worthy of a precious stone, and only then did it occur to me that I had eaten the moon. I had a loaf of bread in my hand, on which I had put the moon (or was it a boiled egg?). I folded the bread and started to nibble it until I had finished it. I didn't dare look upward afterward. Dark settled in, and I concluded that the light of my life had disappeared with the eaten moon.

I stretched out on a stone bench, not far from the wall with the chink looking out over the street. It was shaded by a tree with flowers like orange bells, whose presence dominated a scene from which green leaves were absent. A familiar voice rang in my head, telling me that the tree was called a bombax and that it flowered before it became green again. I don't know where this piece of information came to me from. I was just aware of a warmth deep inside me as if a moon was lighting my inner darkness.

At that moment, I touched my paper essence. I wasn't that "hopeless," "useless" fellow who inhabited the words of my mother, Layla, when she directed her curses at me; then again, she wasn't my mother at all.

The moon that had settled deep inside me told me this, and a lot more. It urged me to ignore the headache, the heartburn and the nausea. It returned me to my identity and to a past dream of which I was both the subject and the dreamer. A dream that some of you may perhaps have come across between the covers of *The Great Interpretation of Dreams* attributed to the Imam Muhammad ibn Sirin, without being bothered about who saw it and told it to al-Hasan al-Basri.

In that faraway vision of mine, I witnessed angels plucking jasmine from the orchards of Basra, and the imam explained my dream as meaning the disappearance of the city's ulema. I felt guilty, as if it was I who had brought them this fate, or even as if I were their murderer or the angel of death sent to harvest their souls. I didn't tell my sheikh and imam that the dream had kept coming back to me for some time and that I had seen bushes stripped of their flowers and jasmine beyond counting covering the paths and trampled underfoot. Then Basra appeared to me, with no jasmine and no orchards, as a sterile, lifeless space, the mere recollection of which frightens me.

I was a human being, with flesh and blood and nerves. Then my vision found a place for itself in the book attributed to Ibn Sirin, and I became a paper being. Recently, I have taken to observing myself, frozen in the form of letters and words between the covers of the book, and I am sometimes overcome by pride, and at other times consumed by indignation.

I never found out who took note of my vision and recorded it, but I do know how my sheikh reacted to it. So long as I live, I will never forget the way he bowed his head at first, nor his subsequent silence. The moment is engraved on my soul, exactly like the paths of my eternal city, with its squares and its sky. Anyone who says that the sky is the same everywhere is a liar. Anyone who says so has never seen the sky of Basra, or completely immersed himself in watching its clouds and mists and their varying colors.

My soul escaped from the prison of the body and I was buried in a forgotten spot at the edge of a vineyard close to the Shatt al-'Arab. I now realize that several feelings came over me successively in that resting place of mine, and that

I was stoking my anger and feeding on my memories, but I continued to remain (I will not say to "live") in *The Great Interpretation of Dreams* attributed to Muhammad ibn Sirin.

Then I appeared, somehow, in al-Minya, a quiet town on the banks of the Nile, to a father who lived as his moods dictated to him, and a mother who was not satisfied by anything, and who could spend the whole day moaning and complaining, until the father emerged from the shell of his silence and answered her with an offhand sentence that would only make her more furious. This was before he finally left us and took to wandering abroad, after spending most of his days—for as long as I was aware of his existence—roaming around the towns and villages of Egypt.

My father loved the art of storytelling and was fascinated by the *Sirat Bani Hilal* in particular. He would follow the reciters around the villages and adjoining hamlets, leaving his work and depriving us of the few pence that would barely feed us, so my mother would glue herself to a Singer sewing machine in order to keep the heater in her kitchen alight, as she used to say. The fact is that my mother's kitchen, small though it was, was the best spot in our house.

When I was a child, I used to like to sit on the marble top, watching her as she cut the vegetables or cleaned the chicken while she spouted curses whose meaning I could not divine, even though I knew quite well to whom she was directing them.

At those times, I liked to surprise her with my favorite question about the identity of my real parents, then jump up and race out of the kitchen while she pursued me with abuse. When she was extremely angry, she would chase me with the intention of hitting me, while in her rare moments of good humor she would content herself with her favorite sentence: "We found you at the door of a mosque!"

She definitely relaxed as I grew up and no longer nagged her with this question of mine. Perhaps she even thought that I had stopped being preoccupied with the subject as I matured. What she didn't understand was that the passage of the years had ripened my preoccupation, but I had become inclined to dissimulation. I hid it from her, first, in order to lighten her misery after my father had first left home, then left the country completely, and secondly, because I no longer needed an answer to my question; for the answer had reached me, in time, in the most direct way, in that I had become completely conscious of my identity.

I became a human being again, though my paper past pursues me and refuses to leave me, like the details of my life in the city of imams and language and orchards, when my name was Yazid Ibn Abih and not Hisham Khattab.

Basra was, and still is, my constant place of return, the dwelling place of my soul, and the earth that I would like to embrace my body and feed on it on the day my spirit leaves me again. It has stayed in my memory wherever I went, and now it is present in my imagination like deceptive ruins that refuse either to disappear or to dazzle, preferring to remain in a state in between.

In my moments of doubt, I remind myself that I have never visited it, never set foot in its streets, never been near the road to the Mirbad or enjoyed the sight of its horizon or its orchards, or even known whether they were full of jasmine or not! But I come back to my certainty that time is a gushing river and place is an illusion. Our true place is the homeland of our souls, and my soul is stuck there in the old city before its subsequent destruction in the Zanj rebellion.

No one would believe me if I told them that my Basra, at once familiar and sharp as a sword blade, has started to appear to me so that I can almost see it with my own eyes. It does not visit me in dreams but spreads itself before me while I am awake, in moments when I am at the limit of my concentration and inattention together. Moments when I sharpen and polish my mind, directing it only to my past in my beloved city and driving it from my present so that it disappears in nothingness. Only then does the city of imams and language and orchards materialize before my gaze, emerging from a white mist that peels away to reveal one of its features. I immediately recognize it, and in those moments, I swear I almost experience how Jacob felt as soon as he realized that Joseph was alive and well and had not been eaten by a wolf.

The mist clears from my vision and I see myself standing at my Sheikh Hasan's door, in awe wondering about the sorrow in his eyes and soul, and he answers me with words I cannot understand. I saw him bowing his head after listening carefully to my dream and heard him when he said, "Wasil has deserted us." I didn't know whether his tone indicated surprise, or a reproach, or pain mingled with a touch of sarcasm. I noticed Wasil ibn 'Ata', as silent as ever, as I passed him in his usual sitting place in the spinners' market.

I saw my city with flourishing markets, its fruit orchards in full blossom and its gardens full of dates and grapes. Then I saw the Tigris drying up and the marshes covered with sticks of cane and alfalfa and noxious grasses. I saw myself running without stopping, my feet bleeding from the rocks on the path as the blazing sun almost set my head on fire. There was no moon in my world, as if the idea of a moon had disappeared from existence, as if I had swallowed it long ago.

As my old self running took shape before my eyes, I imagined that within me there must be a secret I could not bear, and that when I had run before on that occasion, I was looking for a solution to a puzzle that was keeping me awake.

Sitting now on the marble seat under the bombax tree, the contagion and anxiety of the search made their way to me, and I realized that I, Hisham Khattab, would never stop searching, I would remain obsessed with it, unable to quit even if I achieved my goal. The burden of the supposed secret kept me awake, although I could not put my finger on what exactly it was. So the secret turned into a new puzzle to be added to the first puzzle, the codes to which my first incarnation, Yazid ibn Abih, had tried to crack.

The words of Farid al-Din al-'Attar came back to me: "Stop searching, for you have not lost anything, and stop speaking, for everything you say is just chatter." I decided to disobey him, even though I was convinced by the soundness of his viewpoint.

In a trembling voice, I said to myself, "I will never stop searching, as al-'Attar advised, I will search for one thing in another, I will seek out the marks my self left outside of me in the hope of catching a glimpse of it in what it is not."

2

I usually wake with a slight headache, which goes on so long it makes me feel someone is knocking my head from inside with a hammer.

At the same time, I am surrounded by a smell of jasmine, like a cloud wrapping me and carrying me to a place unknown. The smell does not come from actual flowers nearby; its revelation springs from absence, not from actual presence. I look around me, searching for jasmine bushes, or even sambac or gardenia, but I cannot find any. So I am sure that my hunch was correct—the perfume came from inside me, as if it was the memory of jasmine in a world that had suddenly lost it.

I convinced myself of this because I had never understood how the scent could overwhelm me in the strangest places and times, nor how it was connected with the headache and tension that always accompanied it. Unlike those people who are brought calm and relaxation by the smell of jasmine, it has often left me with an unjustified feeling of unease, coupled with an obscure feeling of wrong-doing and suffocation.

My mother, Layla, used to sow mint and basil in small pots carefully arranged on her balcony. If I had ever asked her whether there was any jasmine in our apartment, she would have looked at me as if I were mad. In her eyes, the world was divided into principles that could not be contradicted, and in her view one of these principles, or scientific facts, was that jasmine, roses, and other such flowers were things that were strictly speaking specially for the comfortably off, who had not a care in the world and had nothing to do with poor wretches like us.

I remember a day when I came back with a bunch of carnations I'd bought from an old woman on the corniche beside the Horus hotel, for no other reason than that I wanted to help her. The woman refused to take my money unless I took her carnations, so I gave in and took the flowers back home with me. My mother was coming out of the kitchen, drying her hands on her clothes, at the very moment I opened the door. She looked at me, startled and disappointed, twisting her mouth as she spoke.

"Look at what the crow has brought its mother! Wouldn't it have been better if you'd brought with you two bundles of watercress?"

"Good evening, dear mother!"

She didn't answer me but continued on her way to her room, then slammed the door shut behind her. I looked for an empty bottle, which I half-filled with water, put the flowers in it, and left it on a table in the hall. The next morning, I could find no sign of it. My mother was sitting on the floor, stripping *mulukhiya* leaves, looking at me as if challenging me to ask what had happened to the carnations.

She often said that I was prone to delusions, just like my father, who had been captivated by the Banu Hilal epic. I often heard her lamenting her fate in the kitchen in a voice that was more like a wail. I didn't understand her complaint; in fact I never grasped her relationship to me at all. Sometimes I would look at her and not know who she was. A woman with a lined face clearly etched by sadness, who threatened to burn my books or sell them by the kilogram to the junk dealer if I didn't pull myself together and look for a proper job instead of spending night and day hunched over books with yellowing pages that might fall apart under the pressure of an inexperienced hand.

She wasn't persuaded when I told her that what I was doing was real work and that my books that she didn't like might bring us a lot of money in the wink of an eye. I explained to her that some of these old volumes were rare, that there were people who valued them above anything else, and that my role was to look for the ideal buyer. She would give me one of those hostile looks that in the past she reserved for my father alone, but she didn't say a single word in reply, maybe because I gave her a worthwhile monthly allowance to spend on the house, or perhaps because I had sacrificed my life in Cairo and come back to live with her in al-Minya, fearing she might succumb to loneliness and illness as soon as my father's death in his Libyan exile had been confirmed.

She knew that I made money by selling rare books and manuscripts. Some clients would come to our house and negotiate the price with me while she watched surreptitiously from her favorite spot in the hall, barely believing that there were people who would pay money to buy books with yellowing pages like this. "Useless bits of paper," as she would say.

Sometimes she seemed suspicious, as if the negotiations going on in front of her were just a ruse to disguise something forbidden, like drug dealing or smuggled antiquities, for example. More than once, I caught her examining the volumes piled up in my room, looking in drawers or clothes cupboards for something to confirm her suspicions.

In time, her fears subsided, but she never stopped moaning and complaining. Once she said that the issue wasn't about getting money, but rather how it was acquired, and that she was nervous when she tried to explain the nature of my work to her neighbors, who imagined that I was unemployed.

My mother treated me as if I really was an unemployed person. As far as she was concerned, people were supposed to go to work in the morning and come back at a fixed time. A place of work that was known and whose premises could be visited and boasted about.

Another universal principle or scientific fact, in my mother's view.

She had long ignored the fact that I had no choice about my lack of employment in my specialist field. I loved old books, but they would remain a hobby that I enjoyed in my free time if I could find work suitable for my university degree after graduating. My basic enthusiasm was for the sciences. I loved chemistry in particular. My grades in the general secondary exam didn't allow me to study pharmacy, as she had dreamed I would do, so I decided to enroll in the science faculty.

Until that moment, her hopes for me had not yet been disappointed. She remained interested, thinking about the possibilities with me. When I wanted to enroll in the chemistry department, as I dreamed of doing, she expressed her fears that if I didn't get excellent grades, good enough to be appointed as a teaching assistant in the department, I would become a chemistry teacher in a neglected country school, like thousands of others. She persuaded me, because I didn't like teaching, and at that stage of my life, I wasn't entirely certain of what I ought to do. The solution appeared in a suggestion from a friend of hers to enroll in the geology department, because that would allow me to work in a leading oil company, as her friend's son did.

The surprise was that I graduated with excellent grades. I was the second in my cohort, and I expected to become a teaching assistant, but they contented themselves with appointing just the first in the cohort, while the third was appointed to the science faculty in a new university because his father was one of the university's senior management, while I set out empty-handed on a journey, seeking a foothold for myself in any of the oil companies.

I followed these companies' ads and submitted applications for most of them. At first, I was confident that my excellent grades would easily guarantee me a place in one of them, but with time my confidence began to evaporate. I didn't receive replies from most of the companies, then I received a letter from one of them telling me that I had been placed on their waiting list and they would contact me if they needed me.

I think I am still on that respected waiting list after all those years.

Meanwhile, the son of my mother's friend put in a good word for me at the company where he worked. They told me that I would train with them for just two months in their Heliopolis headquarters. I had imagined I would spend my training period in the desert location where the friend's son worked, but I was left in the company headquarters. I took one free coffee after another, chattering with other trainees or reading a book I'd brought with me to help me through the hours of nothingness. In any case, all my efforts to be helpful to the company were met with a polished indifference.

So, at the end of the two months I returned to my barracks, secure in the army of the unemployed, and my interest in old books grew. They seemed like an ideal grave-yard for me to bury my frustration and feelings of failure and uselessness.

I cemented my bonds of friendship with the Ezbekiyya wall booksellers and stopped telephoning my mother for a spell because she had held me accountable for not continu-ing to work at the oil company and was never convinced that I hadn't been given the chance to demonstrate my abilities to them. They treated my degree, and my excellent grades, as if they were nothing. Almost every position at the company was reserved for well-connected people. While I was there, I saw people come directly from universities to posts that were reserved for them on the recommendations of friends and relatives in the highest positions in the state. My mother couldn't understand any of this. As far as she was concerned, I had thrown away my chance of a secure position in an important international company because I suffered from the same delusions my father did and was simply a loser.

Sometimes I sympathized with her, especially when she gave me a delicious home-cooked meal. Broth with bread and vinegar, lamb with garlic, a dish of macaroni with béchamel sauce, or rabbit with mulukhiya, for example.

Apart from that, I was usually irritated with her, and my feeling of alienation grew. I don't know if children generally feel the sort of alienation I felt toward my parents or whether I was an exceptional case. I always had the feeling that I had been cut from a tree, that I had no roots and that nothing larger would ever grow from me.

I was vaguely aware that I had no mother and no father, or to be more precise, that the only mother I had was one that lived centuries ago, and that I had no father known to me. I totally believed this, and it is preserved in my memory like a nucleus around which all other memories are centred and from which they grow.

In my childhood, I identified with orphans and foundlings, people who lived under the delusion that they were the children of fathers who were not actually related to them at all. I chose to believe my mother's almost constant reply to my question about the identity of my real parents: "We found you at the door of the mosque."

I used to comfort myself by trying to imagine that mosque and imagining myself as a young baby wrapped in a blanket, screaming and crying in a reed basket, yes, always a basket of reeds. But this scenario did not completely satisfy me, for my father and mother, as I knew them, had no connection whatsoever with mosques, and I personally thought it unlikely they had ever been near one. My father never prayed and only woke up just before noon, and my mother never went out except to go to the market or to look for my father.

When I was young, she would always say a single prayer on waking up each day, then listen to the Holy Qur'an on the radio until it was time for the "For Housewives" broadcast on the General Program station, before immersing herself in the household chores, divided between complaints and angry mutterings and listening to a song that caught her attention. And if it so happened that I reminded her of the rest of the prayers, she would point upward and say, "Our Lord knows what is in my heart."

I don't know why I am recalling these details while I am looking through the window at the doorman picking up flowers that have dropped below the bombax tree with the high wall stretching behind it, beyond which is hidden the hustle and bustle of life.

I had woken early, having tried in vain to carry on sleeping. But wakefulness hit me with its heavy fist, and my conflicting thoughts made any attempt to continue sleep impossible. I got out of bed and sat opposite the window overlooking the bombax tree that stirred my imagination.

Were its flowers the color of carrots? No, the color of oranges, or perhaps the color of the artificial flames of my old electric heater in the al-Minya apartment.

Precision is required. It is not a luxury; it is the way to happiness and success. But who will you recite your psalms to, David?

If I use all my imagination, I can almost hear my mother's voice in the distance. It sounds stifled, as if coming out of the hollow of a well. I cannot define the essence of what she is saying. I think she may be humming a childhood song in her forgotten village in the Nile Delta. At the end of the time when I knew her, she had started to prefer ballads that were more like laments. This change occurred after the doctor had told her she had diabetes. She was in a dark mood and started to feel extremely sorry for herself.

No one is like me, as beautiful as the moon.
I am brilliant, people would be guided by my light.

I would hear her chanting in a tired voice, wrapped in sorrow, and be eager to share with her in her lament for her lost youth. When she was happy with me, she would tell me how beautiful she was when she was young. She liked to compare herself to the moon, and I in turn would ignore her given name, Layla, and started to call her "Qamar." She would smile with a contentment that embarrassed her, then tell me off about things that were mostly made up.

16

3

In second-hand bookshops, no one asked me about my academic specialization, or anything else, so long as I could demonstrate my skills in dealing with the details of their own trade. I could recall the different editions of the classics and knew the most important editions of rare books. Knowledge was the most important step for pursuing the forgotten, the lost, and the forbidden.

I am not just someone who looks for valuable books. I have always been an avid reader who wants to get to know the contents of a book before I sell it to a person who is willing to pay a large sum for it. I developed a particular enthusiasm for lost works and took an interest in writers who had filled the world and captured people's attention during their lives, but whose books had been destroyed or burned or lost, so all that was left were their titles, the biographies of their authors, and a few quotations preserved in other books.

I shuddered when I recalled that Abu Hayyan al-Tawhidi burned all his works after poverty had forced him at the end of his life to eat grasses and herbs from the roadside to sate his hunger. I imagine him returning one day to his humble home to be confronted by his books, and burning them in despair and revenge because a generation that would leave someone like him in hunger and poverty was unworthy of the treasures he had written.

I praise God that these treasures were actually copied, and that the copyists continued their work unceasingly and saved them from eternal loss.

But al-Tawhidi was more fortunate than others, whose works disappeared from the face of the earth—like those of Ibn al-Rawandi, whose books I aways dreamed of finding. I don't mean the works that some editors and scholars had reassembled on the basis of extracts found in the writings of other authors who had occupied themselves in answering him and refuting his opinions; I mean his actual books, as he wrote them.

In my daydreams, I used to paint scenarios in which I would find "The Crown" or "The Refutation" or "The Emerald" or "The Pearl," then quickly awaken from my dreams to a reality in which there was no place for al-Rawandi's books or ideas at all.

For a period, this enthusiasm of mine was shared by someone who helped me a lot, so that I regard him as my first mentor, someone who trained me to wander in the labyrinths of rare books. He had an encyclopedic knowledge of the books of the Arabic heritage, a deep understanding of the various Islamic sects and schools and intellectual groupings, and could separate the wheat from the chaff.

He himself had written things, most of which were forbidden to circulate, and an al-Azhar sheikh had declared him a *kafir*, which led him to adopt a secluded and cautious social life, though he remained active in general intellectual debates. Journalists consulted him when they wanted a controversial opinion that would provoke an argument on some topic or another. He had learned from bitter experience only to broadcast his opinions to a few journalists and media experts whose seriousness he trusted.

At first, I followed his weekly essays in various left-wing opposition papers and would feel my mind light up. I would try to read everything I could lay my hands on about the philosophers and intellectual schools mentioned in his essays. I read about the Mu'tazilites, the Murji'a, the Ibadis, and the Ikhwan al-Safa' for the first time, and in this way I made the acquaintance of Ibn al-Rawandi, al-Ash'ari, Ibrahim ibn Sayyar al-Nazzam, 'Amr ibn 'Ubaid al-Bab, and others. As for Hasan al-Basri, Wasil ibn 'Ata', and al-Jahiz, I had known them since I first came across their names in school texts. I was, and still am, enchanted by al-Jahiz, and mesmerized by Wasil ibn 'Ata''s sermon without any R's when we studied it in the second year of secondary school. My colleagues protested that it was too difficult when our Arabic language teacher made us memorize it, but I learned it by heart of my own free will. When I had done so, it seemed as if it was part of my life and my history, but I didn't attach much importance to the matter. I had long been able to memorize classical poems and texts with a facility that always astonished my teachers.

After reading the essays of my future professor, whom the sheikh who declared him an unbeliever liked to describe as a heretic, I tried to meet him despite the anticipated difficulties. The paper refused to give me his address or telephone number and the security man looked at me suspiciously.

I didn't despair but contacted a young journalist whom he trusted and was allowed to speak to him. I met the man in the Cap d'Or Bar downtown. We had each finished seven bottles of Stella and talked about all sorts of things before he trusted me and gave me the phone number of the "heretic's" house—he too called him by this nickname, but with obvious affection.

The nickname sounded nice when it was used with pleasure and affection, and I in turn adopted it to refer to the man.

I telephoned him the following day and was met by a dry, hoarse voice that sounded like the result of decades of smoking. He didn't seem to appreciate my enthusiasm or the words of praise I heaped on him. I told him I wanted to meet him to talk about something that could not be put off. He apologized, saying that as he was nearly seventy, he no longer went out except when he had to, and he could only open his house to a select few people he had known for years.

As I persisted, his voice began to soften. He asked me to leave my photograph, telephone number, a copy of my ID, and a reference from the journalist who had given me his telephone number at the information desk of the paper he wrote for. I thought he was joking, then became convinced he was serious when he continued talking and explained that these papers would be delivered to him at home. Then, once he was satisfied with their authenticity, he would contact me.

I did what he had asked and waited for him to call. His caution seemed excessive, but it made him seem more mysterious and I became more attracted by his personality. At first, I believed that it was enough for him to ask the journalist if I had got his telephone number from him or not; then, when I visited him and saw for myself the isolation that he imposed on himself and his family, I realized he was simply dealing with having been declared a kafir with the seriousness that it deserved.

On the way to his house, I could not imagine what awaited me. I was overflowing with anticipation and curiosity. The man represented an exceedingly complex mixture. He was an Azhari sheikh who attacked the al-Azhar so much that he was accused of atheism and disbelief, a leftist who tried to reconcile the principles of Marxism and what he called the seeds of socialism in Islam, an intellectual who expertly excavated what was forgotten or passed over.

For myself, I expected to meet a heretic like those in the downtown bars, who were full of themselves and of their ability to offer views that differed from the prevailing sentiment. I knew that the man was more complex and cultured, so I expected that he would do this in his own way, with polish, perception, and sophistication. So I was surprised when I entered his apartment on the second floor of a building in the Korba quarter of Heliopolis for the first time. His street was quiet and silent. The apartment had two doors, one opening onto the hall and rooms—or so I imagined, as I never, ever went in by this door—the other leading from the stairwell to a guest room prepared for visiting strangers like me.

The room was furnished with an old-fashioned set of furniture with sky blue covers. The walls had verses and short chapters of the Qur'an hanging on them, including the Throne Verse, the opening Fatiha, and the Verses of Refuge.

The gentleman received me in a dark jilbab, over which he wore a brown coat, with a cook wood rosary in his hand, to which he made mumbling noises that I could not make out. After about half an hour, I heard a gentle tap on the door that joined this room to the rest of the apartment. The man got up, half-opened the door, and took a tray of coffee from a veiled woman, most of whom remained outside my field of vision. I couldn't tell if the woman was his daughter or his wife because of her black *niqab*, which revealed nothing about her.

Despite his intellectual openness and ability to put forward the most stimulating and provocative ideas, he seemed at least as socially conservative as those who condemned him as an unbeliever.

In order to gain his trust and persuade him to have confidence in me, I set out those ideas of his that I liked, and recited Wasil ibn 'Ata''s sermon in full, since I knew it, and still do know it, by heart. He seemed to enjoy my efforts to appear intelligent enough to have the honor to be a student at his hands.

When I had finished, he asked me, "Have you finished all you have to say, Master?" The sarcasm inherent in his question was not lost on me, and I did not know how to answer. I was afraid that any reply might anger him, so I simply nodded my head.

"Wasil was much greater than to be confined to his oratorical abilities, or to his lisping R, which people who have wanted to distract attention from his ideas have concentrated on."

Again, I nodded my head in agreement without understanding exactly what the professor meant.

Going to his house in Heliopolis became a weekly ritual that I could not do without, and I was happy that he was just as attached to this appointment of ours as I was. I realized this when I was suddenly forced to make a journey to visit my mother in al-Minya without being able to inform him. I thought I would be back in good time for my appointment with him, but the train was canceled, and I only reached Cairo at midnight that day. My cell phone had run out on the way, so when I got home I attached the phone to the charger, lay down on my bed, and woke up the next morning. When I turned the phone on, I was surprised to find ten missed calls from my professor. I called him immediately, and he seemed disturbed, only calming down when I recounted what had happened from the time I left Cairo until I returned. He asked me to pass by his house at once, and that is what I did.

After that, our relationship grew closer. He started to rely on me to provide him with the old documents and manuscripts that he needed. He introduced me to the experts and dealers he dealt with, and I became the intermediary, or rather the postboy, who delivered to him what he needed from them.

He confided to me that the fewer people came to his house, the better it was for him and his family. In time, I discovered that his sense of security was higher than I had anticipated. Whenever I entered his house, he would interrogate me as to whether I had noticed anyone following me, if there had been any suspicious movement in the street or an unfamiliar face in front of his house. I would reply with a confident denial, as I repeated to myself, "My dear heretic, the street, any street, is full of unfamiliar faces. That is a part of its nature and its definition."

Deep down, I was certain that no one was planning to assassinate him, for despite his importance and the depth of his culture, hardly anyone outside of his own specialty knew him, and the number of readers of the paper where he published his essays was no more than a few thousand, most of them belonging to the left.

I didn't tell him this, of course. It was impossible to change a conviction that had lodged deep inside him for decades. I noticed that a constant feeling of being threatened formed a deep-rooted part of his temperament, as if an earthquake was about to strike his world. It was easy to increase his feelings of doubt and suspicion and apprehension.

During that chaotic stage of my life, I got to know Bella. I feel annoyed when I remember her and try to banish her image from my mind. It is enough that I am here, cut off from everything I love. I have no mother here, no old books to relieve my loneliness and lessen my solitude. I move about my room and the bathroom attached to it like a caged tiger, stretch out on the bed or stand in front of the window, gazing at the tree with the orange flowers and the mango grove next to the school in the opposite direction from the high wall. Despite myself, Bella comes to me again, and the sparkle of her eyes shines in my memory as she tells me that she has never seen a bathroom attached to a bedroom before.

I am conscious of time as heavy and frozen. Whenever I hear footsteps outside, my senses prepare for an anticipated confrontation with my housemate. She caught me sleeping under the bombax tree in the morning. According to her, I should not have done this; in fact, I should only leave my room at set times to take a walk in the garden and then go back quickly. If it had been up to her, she would have stopped me moving freely inside the walled villa. Fortunately for her, I hardly left my room. When the doorman woke me, I didn't realize she was there at first. She stood watching the scene without speaking, then, with the corners of her eyes and a slight nod of her head, she had him take me to my room. She followed us to the stairwell leading to the upper floor, then stopped to answer her phone. I heard her tell her mother that she wouldn't be able to visit her in the near future because she was busy with me. As I shut the door behind me, she added that I hadn't been myself recently. Her voice seemed relaxed and free of the usual neutral tone she took when talking with me. I am sure that she had deliberately put off coming up to my room simply to play on my nerves. I shouldn't have bothered with her or waited for her, but I couldn't ignore her supposed comment on my spending part of the previous night in the open. She was certainly extremely angry and disturbed now, but I didn't feel guilty. I simply stood staring outside, trying to distract myself from my conflicting thoughts and from the ghost of Bella, whose reappearance had shocked me since the woman had long since departed from my world.

4

Bella entered my life like a cool breeze moist with dew, perfumed with the scent of roses mingled with sandalwood. We were at the start of the third millennium. The air was stiflingly hot, and the sun had not yet set. I noticed her in the crowd. The heat dissipated, and my choking sensation eased as the sun's fire turned into rays of light.

That is how I felt when I saw her for the first time. She was wearing a long, brightly colored dress, and from time to time she pushed her brown hair away from her neck, irritated by the heat and the sweat, before finally tying it in a ponytail that allowed the beauty of her face to be seen with no impediment.

At first, she took no notice of me, so intent was she (like everyone else) in watching the stream of traffic, waiting for the lights to change after being trapped there for an hour and a half or more. We had all abandoned taxis or public buses in the hope of being able to walk across the closed area and reach a spot where we could board some other means of transportation, but we were prevented from continuing at a following stop, so we stood in dispersed groups, awaiting the end of the nightmare known as the presidential procession.

It seemed clear to all of us that the procession must have already passed, so I didn't understand why vehicles were still being stopped and we were being prevented from walking into 'Abbasiyya Square. The important thing is that I noticed Bella in a spot opposite the International Fair area in Salah Salim Street, standing among a crowd of grumbling people, so I made my peace with the world and wished that we could all stay like that forever. She continued her charming movements and expressions without noticing me as I watched her, oblivious to everything else.

But when I noticed the volume nestling in her hands, I almost forgot her. Her slender fingers were clutching the *Great Interpretation of Dreams* attributed to Imam Muhammad ibn Sīrīn—one of my favorite books. Without thinking, I approached her with a smile and asked her about the book, and when I asked if I could take a look at it, she agreed, though she was obviously surprised by the request.

I flipped through it and stopped for a long time at a dream retained in my memory about some jasmine that the angels gathered from the orchards of Basra. I returned her volume to her, thinking that my meeting with her was a sign that ought to be followed up. When the lights changed, I invited her to share a taxi together downtown, since we were both headed there. She apologized politely, but she did say that she was a regular on Tuesday evenings at the film series held at the Cultural Film Center on Sharif Street, and she'd be happy to see me there.

I'd never heard of this center before, but I started to keep up on its weekly screenings, though I couldn't attend them for a couple of months. I was busy with my heretic friend on some research he was engaged with, and I had been commissioned to help him gather some necessary material and information. For my part, I regarded it as a unique training opportunity, through which I might get to know ("from inside the kitchen," as they say) his method of working and investigating the desolate forests and paths of heritage.

At the same time, the day after I had met Bella for the first time, I began to be visited by dreams that seemed like connected fragments of a related life. I don't say this lightly or on a whim: the dreams really did tell me about a side of the life of someone who lived centuries ago.

In my first dream, everything was normal. I saw myself in the al-Minya apartment, arguing with my mother about some vague issue before angrily leaving the house. I went downstairs, taking care on the slippery stairs and the broken step, and went out through the building's iron door to find that it opened on an open space that I did not recognize. It was dawn in the street, and the world was dull as it awaited a day that had not yet arrived. Despite my surprise, I stepped forward, feeling my way in a place that seemed strange and familiar at the same time.

The ground under my feet was uneven. I looked at it carefully and noticed that I was walking in a plowed field. The field led to a vineyard, with a reed hut beside it, and nearby a jasmine shrub whose white flowers could be clearly seen, despite the weak light just before dawn. The number of flowers piled up on the ground was several times greater than those on the branches.

I stood halfway between the hut and the jasmine, shattered and worried. I felt I had to go into the hut to look for something I did not know. It seemed that my whole life depended on this, but on the other hand my soul was dragging me towards the spot that was covered with dead jasmine.

With some hesitation, I followed the call of my soul. I knelt down and fingered the fallen flowers like someone feeling his own body to check it; then suddenly I burst into tears, my vision became cloudy, and my dream disappeared.

On a following night, I was in Basra, wearing a cloak and a turban as I crossed the marshes in a boat. There was someone next to me listening carefully to what I was saying. His face was not clear, and my words were inaudible. I was like someone who was just moving his lips, though in my dream I knew that I was telling my companion my soul's secrets, and that his replies—despite their brevity—were full of comforting wisdom.

So my visions continued, one after the other, showing me part of the story of a life that had vanished, buried under the rubble of forgetfulness, of someone called Yazid ibn Abih, as if he was me. Sometimes I would see myself weaving baskets and mats from reeds with a skill I didn't know where or when I had acquired it, while on another occasion I found myself buying grilled fish and bread from the fishmongers in the Basra Mirbad and sitting to eat them with my constant companion while we engaged in a furious argument. On a third occasion, I saw myself in Hasan al-Basri's circle, listening with my companion and others to the imam as he threw us a firebrand of his incandescent light.

What surprised me was that in my dreams I recognized the places and names of everyone who was with me, as well as my relationship to them, with the exception of my close companion. I couldn't even distinguish his features clearly, and I hadn't a clue about his name. I only knew that we were hardly ever apart and that he called me Yazid, like other people, and that I would answer him at once.

Those fragments that my dreams supplied me with did not help me; on the contrary, they made me even more confused and sleepless. Sometimes I was afraid of sleeping, in case my dreams showed me things I did not like.

When I started meeting Bella more or less regularly, I noticed that without any intention on her part, she would stimulate my memory and imagination to seize on something I had failed to grasp before. There was a glint in her eyes like the joy of first discoveries. I often saw in her a constantly surprised child. If I said to her something like, "The sun rises in the East," her eyes would open wide in amazement, and she would reply without thinking, "Really?" then look at me as if she were expecting some additional confirmation.

With time, I started to realize that she was often barely conscious of what others were telling her. She was usually thinking about something completely unrelated that they could never even imagine. Her surprise might spring from her sudden discovery that they were there, or from recalling that they were close by, intruding on her world.

At first, I naturally didn't tell her anything about my dreams, and didn't even hint at my problems and concerns. Despite this, every time I met her and we gossiped about topics that had no connection with our private affairs, I felt that I had got closer to the world of my dreams and further from my reality.

Her way of pronouncing my name annoyed me. I never knew why she insisted on lengthening the "I" vowel after the letter ha', so that my name became Heesham instead of Hisham. She, in turn, didn't understand at first why I called her Bella rather than by her real name, Mervat. She thought that Bella must be a previous girlfriend like her, or something of the sort, so I was forced to explain my motive and show her pictures and paintings related to the original Bella. I wish I hadn't!

It's never a good thing to cry over spilt milk. In spite of everything, I feel real gratitude toward her, because she was a bridge over which I crossed to the other side of life. She hardly ever comes into my mind now without making me feel depressed as I spend days, each one just like the other, centred on a neutral room, a tree with orange flowers, and a view over a mango grove next to a school that I discovered belongs to the Japanese community in Cairo. Whenever I succeed in putting the memory of Bella out of my head, the details of that life, which appeared to me in my dreams, resurface. It's true that my dreams are fragmented and full of holes, but what I retain is extremely clear.

I no longer even need dreams to transport me to an era that has passed and a city that was utterly destroyed and another built with the same name near to its original location. It is enough for me to shut my eyes and clear my mind until the memories inside me appear, as though visible, not separated from me by time or place.

I recall many details of a squalid house: windows that were closed most of the time, a tightly fastened bag hidden behind a clothes box. I know al-Hasan al-Basri's circle, and I can almost see Wasil ibn 'Ata', the Mirbad of Basra, the marshes, the palm leaf workers' market and the copyists' gatherings. This detailed picture of a city, with its different districts, its shores, its markets, and its palm trees, cannot be just imagination.

I am Hisham Khattab.

That is what I used to repeat at first, to remind mself of who I was and to refresh my memory and encourage it to work at full capacity, after observing how it tended to fall off when my recent memories were concerned.

Then the name of Yazid ibn Abihi began to come to me quite clearly, and I recalled the old dream about jasmine collected by angels from the orchards of Basra—the dream that al-Hasan al-Basri, head bowed, had interpreted as the departure of the city's learned men, followed by a not inconsiderable silence.

Everything else appeared in my imagination like a mist filling my head and floating inside me. A mist that seemed to have almost emptied my body of its internal organs and taken their place, hiding from me everything behind it.

During the phase when I was drawing closer to the heretic, my master and guide to the unexplored territories of our heritage and its rare books, I asked him if he had ever come across the name of Yazid ibn Abihi in any of the books that discussed the Mu'tazilites and al-Hasan al-Basri or Basra in the second century after the hijra. He frowned before asking me, "Do you mean Ziyad ibn Abihi? But he lived before that." I replied that I knew everything I needed to know about Ziyad ibn Abihi but I wanted to know everything about Yazid ibn Abihi. I added that all I knew about him was that he used to frequent the circle of al-Hasan al-Basri, then later joined the early Mu'tazilites and became close to Wasil ibn 'Ata' and 'Amr ibn 'Ubayd al-Bab, but he remained obscure. Hardly anything was known about him.

My master's eyes twinkled, and he scrutinized me in a way that he never had before. It had often seemed as though nothing could capture his full attention, for his mind was always preoccupied with things that those in front of him could only guess at.

He seemed a little distracted, then peppered me with a string of questions: Where and when had I met the name? Why was he so important, if he was so obscure? And why was I interested in him?

He sounded like a police detective interrogating a criminal. It reminded me of when I had first gotten to know him. I tried to outmaneuver him as far as I could. I said I'd come across the name some time ago, in a book whose title I couldn't remember, and that I had noticed it because I had at first mixed him up with Ziyad ibn Abihi. Then, when I remembered that Ziyad had passed away in AH 53, I realized my error and became more curious to learn more details about this unknown man.

I tried to inject some lightheartedness into my voice, to make it appear that it was my curiosity as a seller of rare books that was leading me on and making me feel that the person in question might be worthy of attention.

The heretic thought for a moment before promising to tell me if he found out anything about this Yazid. I didn't mention him for a considerable period. I preferred to investigate by myself, and praised God that I hadn't gotten bogged down in explaining the reason for my interest in a man who, until that moment, I wasn't completely certain had actually existed at all.

In some way or other, he would not have believed me. He would have treated me like a madman, not like a promising researcher, as he liked to describe me. I preferred concealment, as I always did; it was a trait that was deeply embedded in my soul since I had been a seed in the darkness of the womb.

My heretic didn't broach this subject again until much later. By that time, I had actually discovered many details of the life of Yazid ibn Abihi and their connection to me, which were not certainties, but suspicions, conjectures, and misgivings.

FRAGMENTS FROM THE LIFE OF
YAZID IBN ABIHI

1

"Praise be to God, the everlasting, eternal, from the beginning of creation to its end, sublime in his profundity and profound in his sublimity. Time does not encompass him, nor can place contain him. The memory of what he has created does not burden him; he did not create it based on a previous pattern, but made it arise anew, and leveled it through his art, so he perfected everything he created and fulfilled his will, made clear his wisdom, and proved his divinity. So praise be to him; none can challenge his rule or refute his command. Everything is humbled by his might, and everything is subservient to his power. His excellence encompasses everything; not even the smallest grain escapes him; he is the all-seeing, all-knowing."

I, Yazid ibn Abihi al-Khawwas al-Basri, commence this book of mine with the words of Wasil ibn 'Ata' al-Ghazzal. I do not know to whom I am addressing it, but I have no alternative but to write it down, even though no one else may look at it. It is enough to purge my soul of the filth that has clung to it.

In my shop in the palm-leaf workers' market, I have begun to work like a madman, eager to exhaust my body by plaiting baskets and mats by day and by prayer and devotions by night. Hardly any part of me relaxes in slumber, and in the short time allocated for sleeping I stay awake. I am wary of turning from one side to the other, so as not to disturb the sleep of Mujiba, my wife.

In the shop, weaving palm leaves makes me forget some of my sufferings and sorrows—sufferings that I could not divulge to anyone, even to Malik ibn' Udayy the copyist, the interpreter of my dreams, and my companion in my youth and early years.

I love Basra, my city, chosen by my will and heart. I can think of no other place to replace it, nor imagine myself in any other city. I feel that my body is spun from its palm trees, and my flesh is the product of its dates. Perhaps it is for this reason that I love my job as a weaver of palm leaves, because through it I work with the thing I love best in my Basra, as I make the palm leaves pliant and fashion from them shapes that please me. I don't just mean baskets and mats and other useful household goods for ordinary people; I also mean little toys I weave with palm leaves, which I like to distribute to the children of needy women, who play in the markets or walk behind their mothers from one shop to another.

I sometimes give a free basket or mat to one or another of these women. She can use it or sell it and use the proceeds to buy bread or something else for her children. But what really makes me happy is to see the joy in the eyes of the children as they clutch the palm toys I have woven especially for them.

Only then do I think of myself as a generous person and wish I could have remained the same sincere young man I previously thought myself to be. The happiness in the children's eyes takes me back to my lost innocence. Then I retrieve my expansive dreams and unbridled hopes of previous years. And when I do that, my mind conjures up Wasil ibn 'Ata, not al-Hasan al-Basri, my first sheikh.

Wasil comes back to me because I moved from al-Basri's study circle to that of Wasil, and I followed his path, at least in adopting the principle of the "middle way" and rejecting predestination. I remember having heated exchanges with my companion Malik ibn 'Udayy the copyist because he was convinced by Wasil's teachings, though he preferred to conceal the fact for some time.

I followed Wasil from the time he left al-Basri's circle. As for the copyist, he didn't begin to follow Abu Hudhayfa until after his debate with 'Amr ibn 'Ubayd al-Bab.

But these are side issues barely connected to the substance of what I want to record. I said that I recalled Wasil rather than al-Hasan al-Basri now, because Wasil's life, with all its events and mishaps, is more closely connected to my life and my experience.

During the period when I regularly attended the imam's circle, my eyes were directed towards Wasil despite myself. For a long time, I was captivated by his constant silence and composure. When al-Basri came up with an idea I liked or a sentence that pleased me, my eyes would immediately turn towards Wasil, eager to discover the effect of the idea or the sentence on him; but his placid face, immersed in I know not what, made me even more confused, because it didn't reflect any of the inner thoughts of the man—thoughts I was confident were as blustering and tempestuous as a wind raging through the desert sand dunes.

Outside the study circles, I would also follow Wasil as he sat almost continuously in the spinners' market, where he was keen to get to know the poor women to allocate them money from the *zakat* and other almsgiving.

I can now say that my eagerness to give these women some of my creations and to donate toys I had woven myself to their young children was just my attempt to follow an example established by al-Ghazzal.

Now, a few years after his passing, I know that the day of his death was the most important day in my life, which I shall never forget so long as I live. It will leave Wasil, and everything about him, imprinted in my memory until earth covers my body.

During that period, death was like a specter camped above Basra, as if the city had to breathe its air, like it or not. Death became a flood, harvesting dozens of souls every day. It came wearing the hairshirt of a plague that spared no one. And Abu Hudhayfa was among its victims.

I cannot recall those days without experiencing a tremor that shakes me to my bones. I imagined that the proximity and ease of death in this way would be factors prompting people to piety and faith, but the experience showed how naive I was.

In that period, faces acquired a look of gloom, hope, and despair at the same time. Some people clung to the rope of piety, praying to God to save them or regard them as martyrs if they died. Others lost their faith when their prayers for a relative or loved one to be saved were not answered. Some were unable to understand how mercy and kindness were compatible with all this pain and suffering.

As for me, I was torn between these contradictions. All sorts of passions competed for my soul, with scarcely anything to link them. I was filled with doubts and suspicions. I hated my human weakness and doubted my belief in the denial of predestination. It was true that a man was responsible for his actions and that he had free will rather than being constrained, according to my religious creed, but his responsibility and ability to choose almost disappeared in the face of an equivalent horror.

The plague was a fate that man could not confront or challenge. He would either perish, whether seeking or rejecting eternal paradise, or be saved, not through some skill of his own but because the hand of fate had inscribed him in the list of those to be saved.

I moved between the different parts of Basra as usual, not caring about the danger. I needed to prove to myself at least that I was to some degree responsible for what might happen to me. If the plague struck me, it would be because I had not protected myself against it.

My wanderings in the almost deserted markets and lanes allowed me to see my city in its extreme degrees of weakness and disintegration. Some people left their houses open, as if they would welcome a death from which there was no escape, while others shut their doors and windows for fear that their souls might fly away and ascend to heaven while they were not looking. I listened for a long time in front of the closed houses, but only silence reached my ears. I tried to snatch a glance through the open doors, but I could see only emptiness.

Until a day came—the very day that Wasil was transported to the hereafter on account of the plague—and I dared to enter one of these houses. It was on the edge of the city, outside the range of the plague, so far as I was able to tell. It was a splendid house, surrounded by a garden.

In this house, my life changed—though that is a story I feel unable to tell, as it would require more patience and courage than I can manage. The only thing I can reveal is that, as soon as I returned home, I discovered that Wasil ibn 'Ata' had fallen victim to the plague and died. That night, I was stricken with a fever, which I thought must be the first signs of the plague coming to punish me. I started prattling I knew not what, wishing that Mujiba was there to straighten the bed under me and wash my face and body with cold water, but she was spending that night at her mother's.

The whole time, my old dream was there in my head, and its ghost remained there even when I was awake. I repeated it over and over, as though I was seeing it and experiencing it anew. Countless angels were plucking jasmine, but they were no longer plucking it from anywhere in the orchards of Basra but from the garden of the house I had entered without permission or escort.

2

I was sitting—I, God's humble servant, Malik ibn 'Udayy the copyist, in the circle of Sheikh Imam al-Hasan al-Basri, when Wasil ibn 'Ata', the spinner, established the principle of the "position between two positions." I was a young man, listening in awe to the views and *fatwas* of my sheikh, al-Hasan al-Basri. I was in awe of the sadness that dwelled in his eyes and the fear that lurked inside him. I used to ask myself, "How can someone who possesses all this knowledge and enjoys this asceticism feel fear? How can someone like him be apprehensive of Hell or the tyranny of authorities?" I had long understood sadness, but I had never understood fear, even though it was the thing I had experienced most.

I was also attracted by the silence of the spinner. I had never seen anyone who preferred silence to words like he did. During that period, Yazid ibn Abihi was also intent on acquiring knowledge at the hands of al-Hasan al-Basri. We were linked by a companionship that stemmed from being pupils of a single sheikh as well as by a love of dreams, he as the one who received them and I as the one who explained them. During that first period, however, I was not the one to explain his dreams; rather, I would listen as he related them to al-Hasan al-Basri, even if the latter didn't offer a complete interpretation but merely a summary. Who was I to correct my sheikh and imam? I kept silent, certain that our sheikh must have had a good reason to refrain from revealing all the meanings of Yazid's dream to him, just as I refrained from telling him how skilled I was in interpreting dreams and visions. Until then, that had been my own personal secret. I could savor burying it inside me and enjoy slowly maturing it, perhaps in the same way that Wasil ibn 'Ata' developed the Mu'tazilism doctrine in his mind during his long silence in al-Basri's circle.

I spent my childhood and youth intoxicated with the idea that I was living at the center of civilization, since I could see that my city was the axis of the world, in which history was written, skilled minds swayed back and forth, and hearts quivered in anticipation and excitement. How happy I was to be living at the same time as al-Basri, Wasil ibn 'Ata', Bashshar ibn Burd, al-Khalil ibn Ahmad al-Fara-hidi, and Abu 'Amr ibn al-'Ala', and that I belonged to the same city as they did.

At that time, I was naive, elated, and immune to the sur-prises of destiny, confident that fate had in store for me only good things and convinced that my name would inevitably one day appear among these scholars and imams. Armed with my innocence and good opinion of myself and of the world, I started to imbibe all the science and knowledge that

I could. I loved learning at the hand of anyone who could teach me even a single letter. I trained myself not to advertise my talent in interpreting dreams except at the right time. I awaited the time of harvest, and I missed a crucial point; I hardly ever dream, while Yazid ibn Abihi's sleep is soaked in dreams, most of which are fulfilled.

I was saying that I witnessed Abu Hudhayfa the spinner's announcement of his belief in the "position between the two positions," but then my brain becomes confused, and every source takes me a long way from what I really want to say. My purpose and intention here is this decisive moment in my life and the life of many people I knew, even if they did not realize that it influenced the course of their lives to such a degree. It suffices for me to understand—and I take refuge with God, who is free of every fault, from the word "I"—the influence of that moment.

We were in the circle of al-Hasan al-Basri—may God exalt you—when a man came to ask the imam of religion about those who had committed great sins, whether they were unbelievers who had seceded from the Islamic community, as the "Wa'idiyya" of the Kharijites believed, or did a great error do no harm when accompanied by faith, as the Murji'a believed? Before al-Basri could reply, Wasil intervened, announcing that his opinion was that the committer of a great sin was neither a total believer nor a total unbeliever, but rather was in an intermediate position, neither a believer nor an unbeliever. As soon as he had given this reply, he withdrew us to one of the pillars of the mosque.

I, like everyone else, was surprised that Abu Hudhayfa had replied before Imam al-Din and contradicted his own view that the committer of one of the great sins was a hypocritical believer, though I did not pay much attention to the matter at the time.

I began to pay some attention to it, when 'Amr ibn 'Ubayd al-Bab had sided with al-Ghazzal despite the fact that he previously used to make fun of his new sect and his long neck. Wasn't it he who had said, "This man is no use, he has such a long neck?"

I attended the debate between them and witnessed how the Bab withdrew and acknowledged the opinion that al-Ghazzal had put forward. Like 'Amr ibn 'Ubayd, I was struck by the eloquence and clarity of logic of al-Ghazzal, and of his ability to persuade. I started secretly to repeat after Ibn 'Ubayd al-Bab, "There is no contradiction between myself and the truth. I admit that you're right, so let anyone present testify that I have surrendered the opinion I used to hold, concerning the hypocrisy of the committer of the great sin belonging to the people of prayer, and agreed with the opinion of Abu Hudhayfa, and that I have abandoned the doctrine of al-Hasan in this matter."

'Amr ibn 'Ubayd al-Bab proclaimed it openly and took the side of Wasil immediately, while I kept it to myself for a while. Then my interest in the Mu'tazilites grew, together with my feeling of being closely connected to them, when I became aware of their views on the rejection of fate and the rejection of the idea that God, may he be exalted, has characteristics.

When I recall this after all these years, I feel that this argument is particularly my own, and that that period of time, with its fluctuating ideas and differences, was a framework for my personal story, clarifying and illuminating it without any need for explanation. I had committed grievous sins and fallen into a position between belief and unbelief in the view of the Mu'tazilites, but I had not left the company of the believers, even though I am counted a hypocrite in the view of Imam al-Din al-Hasan al-Basri.

Like the Mu'tazilites, I believe in denying fate, since I alone am responsible for my deeds and sins. I could have resisted temptation and followed the straight path that appeared to me, clear and bright, but despite that I deviated from it and gave in to temporal lust that made me lose my mind for several months, which I spent drunk, not knowing where I was or what had come over me. I was like someone out of their mind, determined to expose their shortcomings.

The idea that I was directed by divine will and not given a choice might give me a little comfort and relieve me of some responsibility, but given my deep belief in the denial of predestination, I regard the idea as self-delusion, no more and no less. For I am the one who has subjected himself to misery, put himself in torment and punishment, and brought ruin and destruction on himself.

I can hardly believe—my God preserve you and keep you from error—that a fleeting moment in the past could change a life completely and shift a frugal worshipper from the category of the faithful to that of the unbelievers, or to the halfway house. This is something that is unimaginable and incomprehensible.

Let none of you think that I moved from positions of probity to positions of error only when I looked lustfully at Mujiba for the first time. On the contrary, that momentary lapse of mine had its seeds in an earlier era. It began when jealousy of Yazid ibn Abihi slipped into my heart and I did not resist it; on the contrary, I allowed my heart to nurture it and let it grow, so that it turned into hatred and anger, even though I was arrogant and claimed the opposite at the time.

Now that everything has passed, I think that I was foolish and naive even in my jealousy, since I was not aware of my hidden power and abilities. Yazid needed dreams to prophesy the future but wasn't able to interpret them on his own. For him, they remained closed symbols that needed me, or someone with knowledge like mine, to interpret them and give them meaning. As for me—and I take refuge with the all-hearing, all-knowing one from the word 'I'—I would conjecture many things and events, and they would actually happen without the intervention of dreams. I guessed, for example, that the reconciliation between Bashshar ibn Burd and the Mu'tazilites was temporary and would not last. Bashshar was formed of different material from them. They were people of philosophy and ideas, while he was a man of emotion, led into unexpected lands by poetry, which he followed without hesitation or fear. Poetry was his guide and leader, a stick to lean on in the long night of his blindness.

When I heard his verses praising Abu Hudhayfa's superiority over Khalid ibn Safwan and Shayb ibn Shabba in the speech with no r's that he improvised before the governor of Iraq, 'Abdallah ibn 'Umar ibn 'Abd al-'Aziz, I was certain that verses of satire would inevitably follow, and I was right in my belief.

For after:

*They turned to speaking, and the people congregated /
and penned speeches, (what excellent speeches!)
He stood up and improvised, and his oratory flared /
like the blacksmith's forge, when it surrounds the flames*

came:

*Why should I follow a spinner [Ghazzal] with a neck like
the neck of a desert ostrich, whichever way he turns,
The neck of a giraffe, what do I or you know? /
Will you declare unbelievers men who have declared
another an unbeliever?*

They used to frequent al-Hasan al-Basri's circle together, as Yazid ibn Abihi and I did, but in relation to us they were in the position of a sheikh to his pupil. Yazid and I were the youngest members of the circle of Imam al-Din during that period. And just as al-Ghazzal and the blind Bashshar split up, I split from Yazid after some years of affection and companionship. But even though Wasil declared Bashshar an atheist, and the latter satirized the former, their differences remained intellectual and theological. In the end, it was not Wasil who banished Bashshar from Basra, but ʿAmr ibn ʿUbayd al-Bab that did it. As for what happened between Yazid and me, this can be classed as assassination, treachery, and a series of blunders.

My intuition did not tell me this at first. My intuition was eloquent and vocal in relation to others, but blind and silent to the point of dumbness in everything concerning myself. In my long old age, for example, my intuition would be energetic whenever I saw that young boy who sold grilled fish and bread with his mother. Something about him would sharpen my senses and rouse my energies. Quite early on, I was certain (without any doubt) that he would be very important. The glint in his protruding eyes, which stared with such concentration, told me that he was the sort of person who could survive and overcome the barriers of time and place.

I saw no one to challenge him in his love of books or his interest in reading and writing. As I grew older, I saw my conviction fulfilled that he was unique in his time. I did, and still do, value him and exalt him, and I praise him if I hear anyone tell lies about him. I have lived to witness someone who wished to exchange reading his works for the bounty of paradise, for their company is enough for him to feel he is in paradise. I heard with my own ears someone condemning him for his dark skin and protruding eyes and ugly appearance. That idiot does not realize that in intelligence there is a beauty unequaled by any other beauty.

I say that my intuition often betrayed me and deserted me in everything concerning my future. But its greatest betrayal became apparent when it made me imagine that I would one day be on the same level as Wasil ibn 'Ata' and 'Amr ibn 'Ubayd al-Bab. This was like a deceptive flash of lightning with no rain. It was not my destiny to ever attain this position, and neither Yazid nor Mujiba nor anyone else was to blame for that. The blame lay with the material from which I was hewn. Everyone is made of a cloth that differs from that of others, and my cloth was torn in more than one place.

I don't mean by this—God forbid, may his praise be exalted and his names be hallowed—that there is a defect in the way God created me, or that I was compelled or directed, I mean simply that I never lost an opportunity that came to me to weaken the fabric of my intellect and fill it with holes and tears. Through my will, my impetuosity, and my stupidity, I carved out my path and buried it under pebbles and thorns, so who am I to complain of the difficulty of the path?

For a long time I have been fascinated by the papyrus and reed clumps surrounding Basra. I used to gaze at them as I crossed the marshes in a small boat with Yazid ibn Abihi. I listened to him whispering in my ear things that had lodged in his memory from the dreams of the previous night. I could almost see his dreams, almost fill myself with them, as I translated them into their appropriate interpretations. What I aspired to undertake was a continuous translation of what appeared to him and to others.

Praise be to God, as He is worthy, exalted above the praise of those who shower him with praise. I am content with his judgment—even if my vision is cloudy and his wisdom (may He be exalted) is hidden from me—that I, the interpreter of dreams, should be deprived of dreams. My sleep is a series of unconscious spells, from which I wake like someone returning from the dead.

I didn't know at that time whether I should be angry with Yazid ibn Abihi because he enjoyed this characteristic that brought him close to the status of a prophet or pity him for the misery it brought him.

I am distracted from him on the surface of the marshes that appear before my eyes, but he does not notice my distraction. He gives me a look of one who realizes that his life hangs on a word I may utter. I buy some grilled fish and bread from the fish sellers scattered along the Basra shores and we sit to eat close together. He tells me about his day in the palm weavers' market and I tell him about my day as a copyist of books and manuscripts. I tell him about my annoyance when I find myself forced to copy works that are nothing but rubbish, and my enthusiasm and keenness when I am entrusted with copying an intellectual work. Then I feel that I am almost sharing with the author in his work of creation.

Yazid listens to me carefully as he eats, then tells me that weaving palm leaves is in his view a sort of creation and that he occupies his mind during weaving either by remembering God and asking for forgiveness or by thinking about intellectual matters of the sort discussed in the circle of Wasil ibn 'Ata' al-Ghazzal.

I don't reveal to him that I am keen to write something in the near future. As usual, I conceal the important things, not from a lack of trust in my companion, but simply because anyone who grows up in a certain way will grow old in the same way, and life has taught me to conceal my views and ideas since I was a child.

After we have finished eating, Yazid tells me the content of his dream the previous night and asks me for an explanation of various symbols. He seems happy as I explain things to him on the basis of what is recorded about them in the book of God, may He be exalted, or according to their linguistic basis. His eyes wander far away, and I detect in them the yearning of a child whose overriding quality is innocence.

He says he is fortunate to have been born in this city at this time. He looks toward the east and his eyes mist over with a sudden sadness. I guess he is trying to visualize the places his mother came from. He wasn't absolutely sure about whether her real birthplace was Khorasan or Sind.

3

I, who seek God's forgiveness,* am the worshiper of God Abu Hudhayfa, Wasil ibn 'Ata' al-Ghazzal, the spinner—a spinner of threads, or of words, or of meaning, if you wish. I sit in the market the whole day beside the spinners, lingering with the poor women, to help them.

I remain silent, so people who don't know me think I am dumb. Life has taught me to avoid anything that impedes me, and to shun anything that will not add to my religion. I seek nothing in this life except for the forgiveness of the Lord, may He be exalted.

Malik ibn 'Udayy the copyist asked me to write a treatise for him alone. He said that he would copy it endlessly and hang the original in the window of his shop.
....

* The original Arabic version of this chapter was written without using the letter "R" (or "ر"). The author avoided this letter as a tribute to Wasil Ibn 'Ata' and his famous sermon.

I had dreamed the previous night about the copyist and his friend Yazid ibn Abihi the weaver of palm leaves. We had a day of rain, and it was slippery. There was a she-camel walking before us, and we were following it, but none of us was able to mount her. I was in the lead, with the palm leaf weaver behind me, followed by the copyist, and the path was narrow and slippery. Then the camel lost its footing, landed on its behind, and couldn't get up.

We followed it without trying to help it. The palm leaf man cried and the copyist laughed, while I stood moving my eyes between the two of them and the poor camel, unable to speak. I was no longer suffering from a speech impediment for which stupid people might mock me, but from total dumbness. I had lost my voice and the will to speak.

The words stuck in my throat and I almost choked on them. My two companions were stunned and said nothing. Thay started to stare at me, not knowing what had happened to me. They were used to my saying nothing, but the obvious signs of pain on my face paralyzed them.

Then my grief left me, and I found my voice and my words as the camel disappeared. With my face on the spot where she had slipped, I said to them:

Wake hearts from their slumber! The Mu'tazilite is someone who worships God, is ascetic, and does not pursue or run after lust; he is not full of doubts, nor does he follow the temptations of the soul, which insinuates errors to him. We are worn out by yearning and traveling, yearning and traveling, yearning and traveling ...

When I awoke, the final sentence was still going around in my mind.

I had often been struck by the absolute difference between the personalities of the copyist and the palm leaf weaver. I had never understood what brought them together. I say now: chance, most likely, when they met in al-Hasan's circle, then moved from there to my own circle. Length of acquaintance is sometimes confused in some people's minds with friendship.

One of them was extremely shy, only speaking after a pause and seeming to begrudge his audience his words; the other was gushing in conversation and did not hold anything back, as if the world was his safe house.

For a long time, I had been afraid for the palm leaf weaver, with his excessively trusting attitude. The pair were not among the brightest minds in my circle, but nevertheless they had appeared in my dream a second time. In the first revelation, they were arguing with each other and asked me to act as a judge between them on a matter that did not call for argument or discord.

They didn't ask me about the principle of the "middle position" or about "threat and promise," or anything that concerned us as Mu'tazilites. They were looking at a night sky with two enormous star-like objects in the midst of it. The first of them was a crescent moon and the second a sun, but it had also taken the form of the moon.

They argued about which one of them was a moon and which of them was a sun disguised in the shape of a moon, and their argument seemed loud and violent. I told them what I thought about the two objects, but they took no notice of what I said, although it was they who had asked for a judgment between them. Then the two objects disappeared, falling from the sky into a bottomless pit, and we stood looking anxiously at their empty place in a jet-black sky.

I didn't tell either of them anything about these two dreams of mine, even though the dreams persuaded me to secretly pay them special attention as they sat in the circle of followers around me. Sometimes they stopped at my door, each separately. The copyist would ask for something: he would ask me for a fatwa or for clarification of something he couldn't understand, while the other would bring me something: palm leaf baskets or a mat he had woven himself. If I refused to accept his gifts, he would ask me to donate them to a needy person and insist on not taking them back again.

There is a great difference between the one who asks and the one who gives, even if the one who asks is asking for knowledge. But something about the palm leaf worker made me uneasy, something whose essence I couldn't define. Perhaps it was his unequivocal attachment to what he believed in: an attachment that could defy sagacity and sound judgment, an attachment that was capable of leading to betrayal at any turn because it was blind, with no sense or logic.

Maybe I am wrong, but that was my impression of the palm leaf weaver, although I empathized with him and found him a more attractive person than his companion, the copyist.

In his face and conversation, there was something to be savored, like a bag of musk from which wafts the fragrance of piety and prosperity. A man is where he places himself, and the palm leaf weaver had often placed himself in the circles of knowledge and piety.

On one occasion, he talked to me openly about a dream that had plagued him since his early days, in which angels gathered jasmine from the orchards of our city. He told me how Imam al-Hasan had interpreted the dream to him. My heart missed a beat and I recalled an old dream of my own. I was on the outskirts of the city, scanning the sky, turning my face now to the north and now to the south. I was lost and trying to find my bearings by the stars, like a wise Bedouin, but it was noon and there was not a single star to adorn the sky.

Then I walked in no particular direction until I reached an orchard on the outskirts of my city. At the front of the orchard was a house with a garden whose soil was hard and covered with endless jasmine. I trampled on the jasmine, intending to go into the house. Entering the house seemed to me to be a matter of life and death, as if my life was waiting for me inside.

At the door, I was pulled back by a force I could not identify, then I changed into jasmine, which merged with the other wilted jasmine piled up on the garden paths, and a strong wind came up and carried the jasmine inside the house.

After that dream, I was certain that death would come to me at the time of an epidemic or a war. My soul would ascend to its maker with hundreds, nay thousands, of souls. With every epidemic or disturbance or fight, I awaited my own hour and recited the two *shahadas*, expecting to be among the dead, but the Lord, may He be praised and exalted, allowed me a respite to a new appointed time, for which I am grateful to Him, as I am grateful to Him for everything.

Thus I constantly lived the life of one saying goodbye without revealing this dream of mine to anyone, a dream whose meaning I knew as soon as I awoke from my sleep.

4

Other people look around themselves and see trees or sky, sea or roads, but I, Malik ibn 'Udayy the copyist, see signs and symbols. Nothing is as it seems. What appears is a deception. Some people need sleep to dream, but I dream awake, with no need to sleep.

I see a nightingale, and in it I see a gentle, elegant woman. I see an ascetic in a bat, and in a sparrow a deceitful man. A hoopoe confronts me, and I think of a man who is proficient in his work but irreligious. A dove stands on the citrus tree next to my hut and my mind turns her into a good woman, or fresh news, and a messenger and a message. I am not frightened by the desert, even when I venture into it with no guide, for in my eyes, it is victory and profit and prosperity.

I love Basra, for in my opinion it is *the* city, with the definite article, and the city is security and entrenchment. Didn't Shu'ayb say to Moses, when the latter entered Midian, "Don't be afraid! You are safe!"?

In my Basra, then, is safety and deliverance.

Does someone like me need dreams? My life is a dream, from which I shall awaken with my death. I am not an interpreter of dreams. I live by them. I breathe them, I touch them, I stumble on them wherever I am headed.

Dreams strengthened my relationship with Yazid ibn Abihi and were an opening through which Mujiba slipped to me. I should have guessed that she was determined to seduce me, when she surprised me by visiting me in my hut that morning, eager for me to explain to her a recurring dream. I didn't ask myself why she didn't use her husband as a messenger between us. I was captivated by her smile, even though I pretended to be looking away. She said that from time to time she dreamed she was a well of water at a crossroads through which caravans passed.

I interpreted her dream as signifying riches and wealth. The well beside the roads represented markets from which the passersby could obtain sustenance and goods. After some time had elapsed, I discovered that I had interpreted it incorrectly. Unusually, my passions had intruded and blinded my sight.

The well in Mujiba's dream was not a market or a journey but rather represented an adulteress available for anyone who passed by and wanted her.

On another morning, Mujiba came to me in distress and told me she had seen me as a crow nesting on her window, and that she had been happy and contented in the dream but had woken feeling depressed without knowing the reason. There was no room for misinterpreting the dream on that occasion. I immediately knew what would happen between us, and I did not object to it at all. On the contrary, she became more beautiful in my eyes. I couldn't help myself; I could not control the sudden arousal that came over me. I shuddered with excitement as I contemplated her beauty. I approached her and kissed her mouth passionately, but she evaded me and fled from me with a flirtatious laugh. Her laugh didn't seem to be a lewd one, but strangely, it was tinged with a certain reserve, which was precisely what captivated me.

I didn't sleep for a single moment during the two nights that followed. With the help of God and His goodness, I restrained myself from going to her. I realized that seeing her would weaken the last of my defenses.

During that period, I never thought of Yazid. Mujiba would summon me like a houri deprived of contact with anything or anyone else. I found a substitute in my imagination for the dreams that had always been difficult for me. I started to imagine her with me in my hut and on my bed. I had only seen her face and some strands of her jet-black hair, so I completed the hidden parts of her body with the strength of my imagination.

Then it happened that I woke up from the error I had fallen into. A month had passed since that incident between me and Yazid's wife—a month during which I had deliberately avoided them both and congratulated myself on my willpower. I had taken to staying up at night to recite the name of God, and when her image appeared to me, I banished it by constantly asking God's forgiveness and by imploring the Master (may He be exalted and glorified!) to keep me from the place of those base souls who prefer depravities far removed from virtue. I thought I had made myself sufficiently inaccessible to Mujiba, and it was impossible to ignore Yazid more than I was doing, so I said to myself that seeing her again was the only way to be sure of my success in resisting her enticements.

I had never before desired a woman who was not permitted me. I had averted my eyes and trained my ears to ignore the sounds of temptation in the flirtatious voices of women walking with graceful steps in the markets and squares, but when Mujiba overpowered me all of a sudden, I wasn't ready. At first, I wasn't aware of where her allure was hidden. She didn't seem to be provocative when I saw her face that first time, when I went to their house a short time after their marriage, to take Yazid with me on a journey to a nearby village. I wanted a traveling companion, and I didn't know at that time that my real companion would be the face of his wife, with her slightly shy smile and eyes full of deceitful promises.

A month after she had visited me in my hut, after resisting my infatuation with her, I went to her house on the pretext of consulting Yazid on a worldly matter that concerned me. She told me that he was in the marshes and would not return until nightfall. But she insisted on entertaining me and showing me hospitality until it turned cooler outside, and I did not resist. When she shut the door behind me, I could not help noticing a sparkle in her eyes, and the next thing I knew, I was wrapping my arms around her and drinking the honey of her saliva. She twisted and turned as I held her, but her sighs told me what was on her mind. She seductively threw off her head covering, and her hair, which was as black as the night, fell down over her shoulders as its locks unraveled. This made me lose my mind; I threw her to the ground and mounted her without thinking of the consequences. She yielded to me and hugged me closer; I could not bear it, and my strength dissipated itself on her like an emaciated bull.

She didn't seem disappointed. On the contrary, her eyes shone brighter, and she let out a laugh that I found hard to interpret. I got up from her feeling hurt and ashamed. I adjusted my clothes, waited for a little until I had calmed down, then left her, while she remained lying there, languid and still seductive. Her mouth retained a smile as if she had drunk the very dregs of passion. I now think that I never understood that woman at all.

I went back to her some days later, determined to take my revenge on her. I knew that Yazid was out of Basra, so I crept into her house, taking care that none of the neighbors should see me. She opened the door to me and led me inside. Something in her quiet comportment disturbed me. She seemed at ease with herself, but inattentive to me.

I pulled her toward me and kissed her, and she dragged me toward her bed in the inner room. She helped me to take off my clothes, with a deliberation that teased the nerves, and I undressed her with the same slow movements. There was a look of defiance in her eyes that I could not help noticing.

I responded to her calm with an equal calm. We drank slowly from the dregs of our passion with a total lack of inhibition. When I finally got up from her, she seemed like a cat sunk in torpor and pleasure. No, perhaps she was never like a cat. Something in her made her more like a wild animal. Perhaps it was the intelligence and sparkle in her eyes, or her elegance and vitality.

From that day on, I took every opportunity to pass by Mujiba when she was alone in the house and I could guarantee that she would remain alone for the longest possible time by stuffing Yazid's brain with explanations that required him to isolate himself alone in my hut.

Every time, I told myself that I wouldn't go near her but would make do with letting my eyes feast on her beauty. But I always ended up in her bed, tasting her attractions, intoxicated with her perfume and nectar, so that my appetite for her increased.

Until the day came when Yazid surprised me in bed with his wife. I was naked as I made love to her, quivering between her arms. There was no surprise for her. She didn't even try to show regret or fear. She was cool and collected, while I could not control myself as I hid my nakedness from his startled eyes, which were directed at me and not her.

I expected he would attack her to strangle her or attack me to beat me to death. But instead, he turned his back on us and left, stupefied, with faltering steps. Afterwards, we learned that after wandering the streets for some time, he had headed for the hut and hidden himself there. I agreed with her that he had to be killed, for fear that he might divulge our secret and expose us as soon as he had recovered from the shock.

I beat him over the head with a rock until he was dead, while she stood guard, following me with one eye and watching the road with the other. We dragged him from the hut after digging a ditch nearby, where we buried him and covered the grave with earth. Two days later, I planted a jasmine tree over the ditch that had been filled up and now contained him.

Within two weeks, Mujiba had taken me by surprise and fled Basra, where I do not know. I searched for her with no success, then gave up as my feelings of regret and guilt increased.

I performed my ablutions dozens of times a day and prayed continuously. I recalled the sadness of al-Hasan al-Basri and his fear of the inferno, and said, "Hasan, who never hurt an ant, used to spend his nights awake in prayer, for fear of sins that he hadn't committed, terrified by a hell that he did not think himself absolved from; so what of me, after all the sins I have committed?"

My longing for Mujiba tormented me every night despite my will. I tried to outwit it through *dhikr* and night-time prayers. That was my punishment.

Someone once said, "He threw him in the ocean in fetters and said to him / 'Beware, beware of getting wet!'"—a saying that could certainly be applied to my situation with Mujiba.

With her, I saw the maker in the object, and loved the creator in his creation.

I would sometimes think that she was my means of worshipping and praising the actions of the creator. Then I would think again and ask the all-High, all-Powerful for forgiveness for blaspheming so.

At the end of this process, I felt she was an image bereft of meaning, that I had scrutinized the image and its interpretation had betrayed me. I had been preoccupied with transient things rather than the genuine. I recalled the wide hopes that had seduced me at the start of my life and smiled regretfully, repeating to myself, "The nights and days are pregnant / and none save God knows what they will bear."

I comforted myself with the idea that fate moves on regardless, then I returned to my senses, for it was not right to make fate bear the burden of my sins. From the beginning, I was aware of the dividing line between truth and falsehood, aware of the similarities between the two, and I chose my fate for myself. I walked towards it with my eyes open and a will that was lukewarm about the truth and determined on error.

I had drunk and digested fear from what I had heard about the years when al-Hajjaj ibn Yusuf al-Thafaqi ruled Iraq. Stories circulating about him and others like him had taught me to swallow my words and hide behind silence and ambiguity. I was young, and fear was engraved so deep inside me that it was difficult to pluck it out or extinguish its flames, but despite this I was never able to understand it.

Al-Hasan al-Basri's supplication after the death of al-Hajjaj was often repeated in front of me: "God, you killed him, so take his legacy from us!" I used to repeat that following in Imam al-Din's footsteps, but in my heart of hearts I was certain that that legacy would endure as long as mankind remained on the face of the earth.

I took refuge in concealment, not just to avoid the oppression of the authorities but from everyone else as well. I concealed even from Mujiba what was hidden in my soul, and only gave her the smallest possible hints of how disturbed I was deep inside and of what was consuming me from within. I let her know only of my blazing emotions toward her and my constant yearning for her. How could I not, for the words of Imru' al-Qays applied perfectly to her, when he was asked, "What is the sweetest part of life in this world?" and he replied, "A pretty, fair-skinned girl, well perfumed and well built."

I like to recall my past days—a time of wide hopes and optimism about myself and the world. I try in vain to erase from my memory everything that concerns Yazid and Mujiba. But they are always present with me, each for a reason different from the other. I try to recall the image of the young man that I was at that time, but it eludes me and slips through my fingers. A youth who used to visit cemeteries to learn asceticism and wisdom and ended up as a middle-aged man more treacherous than a wolf.

For some reason that is not clear to me, Mujiba wanted her husband dead rather than abandoned. I recently realized that death had been her goal from the first moment. At first, she went along with me when I tried to persuade her to divorce him and marry me after the months of her 'idda had expired. Everything seemed in order, and my conscience only pricked me lightly at that time.

I wasn't able to look with a clear conscience into Yazid's eyes, which were relaxed and trusting with me, but at least I was more at ease with myself than I am now. The possibility that he might surprise me in bed with his wife never occurred to me because I knew his daily habits and movements through the day better than she did. When he had finished his work in the palm leaf weavers' market, he would sit for a time with our friend Abu Bakr al-Nazzam in the cobblers' market before going to the marshes or to his devotions in my hut, which I left free for most of the day.

He would often accompany me, and when I left him for some personal business of my own, I would take care to find out where he would be, so that I could catch up with him as soon as I had finished my business. Naturally, this concern of mine increased after I had put myself in positions of error and regret with Mujiba.

On the day when he surprised us together, I was confident that he would stay in his shop in the palm leaf weavers' market until late. He was late in delivering a large consignment of mats and baskets, and asked the customer for a two-day extension. On those two days, he worked night and day with his two assistants to complete the weaving by the new deadline.

I passed him by before I went to her and made certain that he was absorbed in his work, to the extent that he hardly raised his head to look at me as he returned my greeting. I said I wouldn't disturb him but would come back to visit him during his short break around evening.

I didn't know that he would shortly afterwards catch me in flagrante delicto, just as I didn't know that this was the last time I would approach Mujiba full of lust and desire, rather than fired with a desire for vengeance and humiliation. If I had known that, I would not have gotten up off her, even if the whole of Basra had stood watching us.

After we had rid ourselves of Yazid, I took her like someone taking vengeance on himself, on her, on life and on everyone, forcefully, roughly, and quickly. I became used to crying on her breast afterwards, when she would push me away and get up from the bed in silence.

She never objected, and never replied when I insulted her and accused her of dragging me to the deserts of sin or charged her with the responsibility for killing Yazid. Only once did I see in her eyes a look of mockery that she quickly suppressed, as her eyes again became empty and free of any meaning.

If I had never properly understood her before that, she became completely incomprehensible to me, in the final days before her escape that was as sudden as the vicissitudes of fate. I searched for her like a madman. I turned over every stone in Basra and the area around it, looking for her. I asked the guides and travelers on the roads between Basra and nearby towns, but no one could point me to a track that I might follow.

Then a man took the bag of dinars I offered and told me that the person I was looking for had undoubtedly died, of hunger and thirst in the Samawa desert, after being betrayed by a guide who had abandoned her there on her way to Kufa.

I almost strangled the man, as I sensed that he was the guide who had betrayed Mujiba's trust. He pulled my hands from his neck and pushed me away, and I fell on the ground, banging my head on some stones.

I was divided between the pain from the fall and the ache of my grief for Mujiba—if she was really the female traveler disguised as a man who had been left to her fate by the guide who had taken his fee in advance.

I stayed lying there for a while, my eyes misted over and

my vision blurred, as if the world had turned dark in front of me and left me completely powerless.

Mujiba had left their rented house two weeks after the death of Yazid. Without any effort on my part, a rumor went around that the pair had left Basra for Kufa after a relative of Yazid's who was living there had died, leaving him a house and a palm grove there.

When I was asked about the truth of the matter, I did not give a definite reply, but contented myself with hinting that Yazid was now in a much better situation than ever before.

My regret at having mistreated Mujiba was greater than my regret for betraying Yazid. Yazid seemed to belong to a bygone age, while Mujiba was my present and my future. But as the days went by, and I continued to despair of reaching her, I was again consumed with regret at my original sin, as I wavered between *dhikr* and nighttime prayers for forgiveness and my secret passion for pleasures I discovered as I awakened their embers slumbering deep inside me.

I married a beautiful, wealthy woman and lived with her in her house, trying to forget my past mistakes. She died and I inherited her wealth; then I married a second time, then a third, and I had more than one slave girl in my possession. I bought Yazid's house from its original owner and was always careful to keep it in good condition.

I no longer resembled the ascetic I had been in any way, even though I kept my old hut, and often went there to perform my devotions and seek forgiveness. From its window, I could see the jasmine shrub that I had planted over Yazid's grave. To guarantee that I would not be disturbed there, I bought the whole of the adjoining orchard.

Staying in that place was like a tax I had to pay for my crime to stay alive in my memory. I was in torment because I was close to the grave of my childhood friend, and this torment was like a coat of thorns with which I had to make my peace and be content.

5

In the space between Basra and Kufa, I almost lost my life. Disguised as a masked man, I left my house at dawn with a bag containing some food and a smaller bag containing some gold dinars and some jewelry—rubies, coral, lapis lazuli, and emeralds.

Kufa was still some distance away when the guide left me in the middle of the road. I had made a mistake when I paid him his fee in advance. I woke at dawn and could not find either him or his mangy camel anywhere near me. I was afraid that he might have stolen my bag and its contents, but I remembered that I had hidden them beneath me while I slept. It hurt my side, but I put up with the pain for the sake of the hoped-for reward. No pleasure without a price, and to enjoy the honeycomb, we must endure the bee sting.

There is no doubt that Malik ibn 'Udayy the copyist understood this all too well after paying the price of his pleasure in a way that he had never anticipated. It puzzles me how extremely intelligent men can lose their minds completely when confronted by their carnal appetites. At first I looked at him in awe. How could I do otherwise, seeing he was someone who had studied with al-Hasan al-Basri before joining Wasil ibn 'Ata' al-Ghazzal and 'Amr ibn 'Ubayd al-Bab's circle? How could I do otherwise, when people traveled from faraway places for him to explain their dreams and visions to them?

When I visited him for the first time in his hut, I really wanted him to explain my dream to me, but I was also in thrall to an overwhelming desire to force him to notice me and recognize me as a woman. This represented a dream that was difficult to achieve, though my wishes pictured it to me as being within reach.

The second time, my hopes increased, especially when I observed the first look of desire in his eyes, followed by a quiver of his lips, and he approached me to snatch a kiss that shook my body because it was like a forbidden fruit for both me and him.

I escaped from him and left him quickly, but my steps grew heavier, urging me to go back to finish what I had begun. I laughed with a mixture of pride and disappointment. I had expected my hunting expedition for him to last longer and that he would refuse me and resist my enticements more firmly.

The dream of the crow nesting at my window wasn't my only visitation on the previous night. Malik was with me as well. He was a guest in my bed, mounting me sometimes with a loud shout, and at other times quivering in my arms or cringing under my feet.

In the dream, he was nicer than in reality, warmer and more elegant. I was his slave girl once and his mistress several times. I woke that day bathed in love juices as never before or since.

When I visited him in his hut, I only told him about the crow nesting at my window. I didn't say a word about the pleasure we had drunk together, but I wanted my dream to be fulfilled as soon as I went into his hut. I wanted him to be kind to me and to give me to drink while awake as he had already done while I was asleep. I hoped he would be like a constant downpour of heavy rain.

How great is the divide between sleeping and waking!

I never understood what brought him together with a person so undistinguished in purpose and reputation as Yazid ibn Abihi. To me, their relationship represented something of a riddle. Then I noticed the longing in his eyes; I was seized with a mixture of happiness and contempt, and I knew that I had the chance to carry out my plan.

It was not greed that motivated me, nor were jewels or gold dinars my objective. I mean, of course they were one objective, but they were not the only one. I wanted to teach Yazid one last lesson. I wanted to take revenge on him for dragging me to a life of hardship and penury at a time when he was secretly amassing a fortune. Did he think that I wouldn't discover what he was hiding while I was living with him in our cramped rented house?

I could have run away with the bag as soon as I discovered it, and I would have done so sooner or later, but the entry of Malik the copyist into my life changed my plans. At one time, I really wanted to live with him after I had left

Yazid and taken vengeance on him, but I figured it would be stupid to give in, as men do, to my emotions and desires. I was smarter than Yazid and the copyist combined, and my sole object of desire was lurking in a bag that never left me. I thank God that I didn't tell the copyist anything about Yazid's treasure. As soon as we had buried the body together, my partner in crime started to complain and wail like an annoying, pampered youth. He started to insult me and accuse me of the most outrageous things, lamenting his fate, which had thrust him into my snares. His feelings of guilt surprised me, as did the way he referred to Yazid as his best friend. Where was their friendship when he was taking his pleasure with me? Did it evaporate as he raced me to break his friend's skull with a stone before he revealed our secret to the world? Why did he only wake up from his stupor and lift his blinker when he was confident that Yazid ibn Abihi was resting under the ground, powerless?

Two days later I followed him at noon and saw him dig up Yazid's grave and leave it open to the sky for a short time before filling it with earth again and planting jasmine over it, then falling to his knees beside it, putting earth over his face, and beating his face as women do. At that moment, all my desire for him disappeared, as if it had never been, and I was afraid that this madness of his would lead to our being exposed.

But what really astonished me was that he knocked on my door at sunset on the same day, and as soon as I had let him in, he fell on me with kisses like bites and dragged me to the bed. He didn't give me a chance to resist or even to speak. He grabbed me by force with a suppressed anger as if he were wrestling an enemy, then wept on my breast as he embraced me. When his eyes were dry, he put on his clothes and left at once.

I was sure that this would happen again and again, and indeed it did. He came to me almost every day, sometimes more than once on the same day, veiled in women's clothes. The day before I fled, he never left my house. Without a single word, he put me on the bed and indulged his lust. Then he got up without looking at me and wandered about the house naked with the windows closed before returning to me. He started to ask me about Yazid's habits and his favorite parts of the house. It seemed to me he had begun to imitate him, as he sat in the spot I had pointed out as the place where Yazid liked to relax, and narrowed his eyes like Yazid did when he was concentrating.

This frightened me. I felt that I was being confronted by the two of them, the killer and the victim, intermingled in a single incarnation. Cain and Abel, with no place for me. I, Mujiba between them. As he left that day, disguised in a woman's dress and burqa, he told me that in a few days' time we would travel from Basra to Damascus, where we would marry as soon as five months had passed since the murder of Yazid. I changed the date of my departure accordingly.

Until that moment, no one had noticed Yazid's absence.

I don't know what happened to the copyist after I left Basra, not even whether he was still living there or had also fled. When I took flight, I was concerned only with my own escape and keeping a grip on a bag that I regarded as an extension of my body, a bulge that weighed me down just as my name had weighed me down in the poor quarter where I grew up.

"Mujiba," after the name of the madwoman of the quarter, the woman about whom it was said that even looking at her would bring madness. How was it that I bore her name? I heard the children running after her and making fun of her and felt that they were insulting not her but me.

I can still see her selling chickens in the market with an inane laugh or arguing with a man in a loud hoarse voice. I pity her and envy her at the same time. Yes, I envied her for her carefree spirit and her lack of attention, or perhaps it was her lack of interest, in how other people saw her.

When someone calls me "Mujiba," I feel I have turned into a madwoman, wandering aimlessly, indifferent to the entire world, unconcerned with everything except the chickens that she rears herself and sells in the markets without having the chance to enjoy the taste of them herself.

I heard someone say that Mujiba's chickens were also mad and never stopped clucking, raising a noise and racing all over the house of whoever had bought them. The lie made me laugh, but a lot of people believed it, and many people refused to buy goods from the poor woman, apart from some kind-hearted souls who bought whatever she was offering despite not needing it, simply to give her some cash to keep her alive.

When I was younger, I witnessed Wasil ibn 'Ata' al-Ghazzal buying things from her and donating his purchases to poor women and widows. He didn't believe that the chickens transmitted madness. He was an abstemious man, eating and drinking just enough to stay alive and preferring to help the poor and needy. I often observed the way he sat beside the spinners in the market to acquaint himself with people's circumstances and problems, to learn which ones needed help without asking them questions that annoyed them, but simply sitting there and weighing them up.

I never reached Kufa. After wandering in the Samawa desert for a period whose length I could not estimate, I was rescued by a Bedouin who conveyed me on his camel to the oasis where he lived. I stayed in a shabby tent of a crippled old woman who needed someone to look after her. I was told that her five sons had been killed during the time of al-Hajjaj ibn Yusuf al-Thaqafi. I said to myself, "Everything will be all right so long as my beloved bag stays with me, to bear the hardships and difficulties of the journey with me." It never parted from me and I hardly ever left it.

The nights passed heavily over me. I often longed for Basra, with its orchards, markets, fishmongers, and bakers on the edges of the Mirbad. I even longed for my old quarter with its madmen and wickedness. Night after night, my determination wavered and I was overcome by cares. The old woman died with no heir, so I lived alone in her tent. I was no longer fresh and pretty as I used to be. The harshness of the desert had dried my body out, and the desert sun had burned my face so that it never regained its former freshness.

As time went on, I opened my bag and looked at the money and jewels, then tied it to a belt I fastened around my waist under my clothes. That was the only way that I could feel safe. When I was overwhelmed by depression, I would finger my waist through my clothes and almost touch my precious treasure. I would comfort myself by saying that I was lucky, despite everything, for at least my crime had not been discovered, and one day I would be able to get to Kufa, where I would buy a house surrounded by orchards on every side—a house in whose garden I would take care to ensure no jasmine was planted or reed hut built.

Until then, I would continue to live in this tent, surviving on donations from the charitable or on the little money I could earn from helping this or that woman with kneading, baking, shepherding, or milking goats. As soon as the sun's heat abated, I would set out on the paths leading to the oasis. Walking on the road relaxed me and made me feel that I had not yet settled and that I was still walking along the road that led to my desired destination.

In my childhood, I used to watch the beaders in the Basra market. I loved beads and beadmakers. I was mesmerized by the colors and the precision of the design. I loved everything made with care and affection. In my clothes trunk I kept earrings and necklaces and bracelets of colored beads that I had collected since my childhood. I gathered pears and quinces and pomegranates from the few trees in the courtyard of our house and sold them in the market. Instead of the sweets that my mother let me buy at a fraction of the price I sold them for, I would go to the bead makers to buy something that they were displaying.

When I married, I would set aside part of the household expenses to buy something appealing from the beaders. On nights I spent alone while my husband was away on some business, I would inspect my collection. Its existence consoled me and alleviated my loneliness and my yearning for I didn't know what. This went on until I discovered what Yazid was hiding from me, in a crack in the wall concealed by the clothes trunk. I used to keep myself from feeling bored and lonely by cleaning and rearranging the house. One day, while I was moving the trunk to sweep away the dust and dirt under it and behind it, I saw the crack and what was in it. It resembled an eye gloating and mocking me.

Amazed at the sight of the jewels and gold dinars, I wrapped them up again and put everything back as it was. After that, I no longer wanted to console myself with my collection of objects made from beads. Who looks for light from a lamp when the sun is in the middle of the sky?

I waited for Yazid to broach the subject of his treasure, to explain to me his secret, or tell me that we would soon be leaving our life of poverty and indigence, but nothing happened. Most nights, he shut himself away in the reed hut, leaving my revenge and hatred for him to mature over a slow fire, the fire of my loneliness and deprivation.

On the nights he spent in the house, I would hear him moaning beside me when he thought I was asleep. Every time I heard him crying like a woman, my aversion to him increased.

Perhaps if Yazid had been a beader, our destiny together would have been different. Perhaps I would have loved him and been happy with him, even if I had discovered that he was hiding from me a secret as large and dazzling as a treasure. I remember our first days together. He would talk to me nonstop, hardly leaving me unless he had to. He would talk to me about al-Hasan al-Basri, Wasil ibn 'Ata', 'Amr ibn

'Ubayd al-Bab and other intellectuals. I didn't understand much of what he was saying, but I remember my amazement and pride that my husband should be sitting with these people.

My father was a weaver of palm leaves like Yazid, but he wasn't interested in anything outside the boundaries of his shop. He would devote himself to plaiting mats and baskets the whole day long and return when evening set in, tired and exhausted.

As for Yazid, he divided his time between his shop in the palm leaf weavers' market, intellectual discussions in the Basra mosque, and his meetings with friends in the marshes and the Basra Mirbad where the papermakers' and copyists' market was.

He had stopped attending these meetings during the first year of our marriage, before he later rejoined them and performed his devotions in the reed hut belonging to Malik the copyist. In that first year, he taught me to read and write. He was gentle with me and wasn't angry when he noticed my lack of enthusiasm for learning.

As time went on, the veil of ignorance was pulled from my eyes, and the obscurity of the written word began to grow clearer to my sight. I spent my time enjoyably, reading manuscripts that Yazid stored with considerable care and attention. He also liked to jot down thoughts and things that had happened to him. His style was too intellectual and obscure for me, but I was eager to study his writing without telling him I was doing so.

Just as I didn't tell anyone at first that I knew how to read and write. A piece of information that in the final analysis wouldn't concern anyone. Then again, it was useful for all of us to keep secrets that concerned no one else. I remember now that Malik the copyist didn't even know that I knew how to read and write well.

There was no opportunity to tell him this. We were busy together with other things.

DAYS THAT FALL APART LIKE THE BEADS ON A NECKLACE

I

In her childhood, Layla heard so many stories about the Nile flood that many of her earliest memories were drowned in waters that were difficult to drain. She used to contemplate the quiet, placid river, astonished at the enormous gulf between the reality and the ferocious image of the Nile portayed in her parents' and her grandparents' tales. On her way to school in the neighboring village, the idea crystallized in her mind that things might differ in reality from how they appeared in stories.

She persuaded herself that the Nile had not changed and that it had never drowned whole villages or ruined crops or killed people. This only happened in stories, to make them more attractive and engage the minds of young listeners.

She would wake up from her sleep and get ready to go to school as Muhammad Fawzi's song "Always in My Heart" blasted from the radio. This song would be broadcast almost every morning at the same time. As time went on, it became part of her memory. As soon as the musical introduction reached her (anywhere and at any time), scenes and memories would rain down on her one after the other. She would recall dawdling until the song ended, the cold of the morning, the light mist outside, and her mother's voice hurrying her on to leave.

She would leave their house built of white stone with the song still reverberating in her head. The neighboring houses were almost hidden from her sight by the magical effect of the mist. She reached the outskirts of the village, where fields stretched away to the right and cemeteries to the left, and thought the mist had lost its magic, for the graves appeared quite distinct while the mist collected in milky clouds in the corridors between them.

She said to herself: death is like disgrace, it cannot be hidden.

She carried on walking, trying to overcome the depression that came over her in the same spot every day.

She didn't know whose idea it was to put the graves next to the houses this way. She pitied the house that stood at the entrance to the graveyard, only a few paces from the graves, then remembered that the house itself was like a tomb, and that the woman living there scarcely left it except to recite the *Fatiha* over the soul of her deceased husband at his grave, surrounded by cacti and basil.

It suddenly occurred to her that the woman, who was always glowering, had no need to go out for this purpose; she only had to open her window and put out her hand to touch the rear wall of her husband's tomb.

She wanted to laugh but she suppressed her urge, for she could almost hear the voice of the mosque sheikh repeating, "For him who takes no heed of death, there will be none to warn him of it."

The phrase made her feel as if she was drowning in a sin for which there could be no forgiveness, for she invited mirth in a place the pious ought to approach seriously and solemnly.

But mirth in her case was just a passing visitor, for what she really felt—every time she passed this spot—was a heavy, corrosive fear, like a rock with sharp edges that wounded her chest from the inside, making her forget every other emotion. She left the cemeteries behind her and took the road that sloped up and linked her village to the earthen embankment leading to the village where her school was situated.

The low-lying position of her village in relation to the surrounding areas often made her feel as if they were living in a ditch below the surface of the earth, or that the village, with its houses, fields, and cemeteries, had been deposited by the Nile: it had once been part of it, before the waters retreated and it had been exposed to the sun; then in time it was inhabited by people who had thought of building their cemeteries before bothering to build houses for themselves.

She stopped, looked back, and saw the village sinking in the mist. The Nile, with its trees and houses and birds, seemed far away, hidden in a heavier cloud that shielded it from her eyes.

She walked on, trying to imagine a new world that might be revealed to her as soon as this milky mist dispersed. She prepared herself to confront her greatest source of fear: the bend almost in the middle of her walk, the spot where the unpaved road twisted like a snake before continuing on its way. In the middle of this bend stood an enormous mulberry tree, even bigger than the one that crouched in the courtyard of their house.

Layla always wished that she could invent a path that did not pass by this "crook," as the people of her village called it. It wasn't so much that she feared it herself but that her body shuddered at the gossip about it, about the mulberry tree, to be precise, and about a ghost who stood under it, raising his hand to touch the top of it and closing off the road to anyone wanting to pass.

The ghost had never appeared to her. She had only heard other people gossiping about it, exaggerating his height and the sound of his tearful splutterings and the way the outline of his gray body merged into the mist. No one knew what made him cry. Everyone came up with their own explanation, and she wavered between believing in the existence of this frightening creature and thinking of him as a fairy tale. She was afraid that if she rejected him, he would take it as a provocation and want to reveal himself to her in his most frightening guise. But she also feared that if she believed in him, he would become a fact that would inhabit her mind forever.

She hurried on, reciting the throne verse and the two verses of refuge in a whisper at first, before raising her quavering voice. But when this did not calm her, she reverted to a whisper as she moved on, almost at a run.

In her first years at school, she and her elder brother

would go there together, but he soon moved on to the secondary school in a more distant village while she continued to wrestle with her fear of the path and its ghosts. She didn't experience any fear on the way back; it was as if she was in another place that was nothing like the misty world of the morning. The sun was shining in the middle of the sky, the colors were bright, and everything was clear—so clear that the ghosts broke up into particles that could hardly be seen and disappeared.

In the middle of the third preparatory class, Layla's mother decided that her daughter had had enough education. She wouldn't give in to Layla's pleas, nor to the objections of the headmaster and her teachers who came to their house to persuade her parents that their daughter was a talented student with a promising future if she continued her studies.

Her teachers' faith in her came as a surprise; none of them had indicated that they had such confidence in her before her mother's decision. She was naturally aware of their high opinion of her and their encouragement of her, but she was not expecting to hear such continuous praise of her intellect and brilliance, especially from the headmaster, who she had never realized was even aware of her existence.

Her mother's head was as impenetrable as the stone from which their house was built. Nothing could change her mind. Even when her husband showed some flexibility under the pressure of his insistent elder son, who was eager for his younger sister to continue her education, her mother would not budge. Sometimes she said she was tired and wanted someone to relieve her of the burden of the house, and sometimes she repeated that her daughter had grown up and it wasn't right for her to be walking alone like that on deserted paths.

As for the girl herself, after her initial tears, and despairing of her inability to change her mother's mind, she started to consider the potential advantages of her mother's decision. The first was that she would not now be forced to pass the frightening "crook" every day.

In those days, she imagined this spot would never let her alone; it would go everywhere with her, including to al-Minya, the peaceful city in the south where she lived after her marriage.

The "crook" would haunt her dreams as well. Even after her days had come apart like the amber beads on a necklace, she still saw herself in her dreams walking toward it, though she never walked past it to continue her walk on the unpaved road, but turned around the tree and went down the slope that led to the lower path, which formed one of the sides of the triangle planted with crops that she could not identify. The path was flanked on the other side by a canal that ran parallel to it, on both sides of which grew camphor and gazorina trees. There was always a light mist and complete silence. She was making for a destination that she was totally ignorant of, her heart beating hard against her ribs.

Her dreams were never of her family home or the streets of her village, or even of al-Minya or their apartment there. There were no places in the geography of her sleep except for that spot, which appeared to her to be squatting in the void, with nothing before it and no life after it.

Hardly a week had passed after she left school when the village was pummeled with rains like no one had ever seen before, even the oldest inhabitants. The rain poured down for five days in a row. At first it was accompanied by thunder and lightning, which shattered trees and tore off flimsy roofs. Then everything else stopped, and the rains continued on their own. Continuous downpours, almost noiseless, except for the clatter on a hard surface or a pool of water that formed in this or that depression.

Everyone stayed at home. Some people were happy because the rain had spared them the trouble of watering the land they had planted with crops; others were afraid of the effect the flood of water might have on their houses, which were insufficiently prepared to confront it. People kept their fears to themselves until a loud cry went up from the entrance to the village, where the graveyards were situated.

The sound was harsh, emotional and jagged, dropping for a time before growing louder again, but the degree of agitation did not diminish. In that long-past moment, Layla felt that the pain and anguish could be measured exactly by an instrument, and that that instrument was her ears.

She realized immediately that the voice belonged to the woman who lived in the house beside the graves. She was certain of it, despite the fact that she had never heard the woman speak. Even when she said good morning to her, and she saw her following the road from behind her half open window, the woman would refuse to reply.

Later, Layla became certain that her hunch was correct. The woman who was always glowering was the first to cry out when she saw from her window that the rain had drowned the tombs and destroyed their tops, leaving them open mouthed, choking on water.

The villagers who gathered there said the woman had hidden herself away in her house again as soon as she was sure her message had reached its intended audience. No one remembered her until after the confusion had died down, as everyone was preoccupied in saving anything they could.

As the rain continued to pour down, there was little they could do except lay wooden logs and planks over the tops of the graves and cover them with plastic tarpaulin sheets. This didn't stop the water getting in but it was something. Most people averted their eyes from the bones floating in the muddy waters. The women lamented the dead as if they had just died, while Layla hid in her bed and covered herself with a thick blanket. Sleep was her refuge, but she found it irksome that day because the incident took place in the morning and she had had enough sleep the previous night. Despite that, she stayed covered up with her eyes closed, like she did when the weather surprised her at night with a thunderstorm, when she would leave whatever she was doing to hide under the covers, praying—once the flash of lightning had passed—that the thunder would in turn stop its clamor.

Her mother had gone with her father and brother to the graves, leaving her alone in the house. She could hear in the distance the muffled echoes of lamentation, and in her imagination she started envisioning various images of what was happening there. The images came together to form a single scene, of a gigantic gray ghost almost hidden in the mist, raising an arm to touch the top of an ancient mulberry tree. The paths in the graveyard planted with cacti and basil vanished from her mind, to be replaced by a mist behind which lurked everything that frightened her.

The following day, the rain stopped and the sun shone. Everything looked bright and clean, so long as one didn't look down at the mud and pools of dirty rainwater. Everyone was busy calculating their losses. They first tried to dry the open-topped graves and collect the bones of the dead. They were confused and puzzled as to whether they should say a prayer over the remains before they reburied them, and if so, what prayer they should use.

The mosque sheikh was not there, as he was from a different village and only came to their mosque once a week for Friday prayers to give a sermon and lead them in prayer. The slippery paths kept them from going to ask him, so they made do with a communal funeral prayer, then rebuilt the ruined tombs.

In his sermon the following Friday, the sheikh spoke about the religiously correct methods of burial and about how the dead should have earth heaped over them rather than having their corpses placed inside tombs that resembled squalid miniature houses. The people listened to him respectfully but didn't make any changes to their tombs worth mentioning. They left them as they were, though they were careful to repair them and reinforce their roofs as a precaution against treacherous rain and storms.

For her part, Layla persuaded herself that what had happened was just a story told to the villagers by the depressed woman. Her shouting was an attempt to attract attention. As soon as the people rushed out to find out what was the matter, she captivated them with her hoarse voice, which slipped through the chink in her window overlooking the graveyard. Somehow or other, she grabbed their attention and told them the story of the rain that had overflowed and flooded the land where the dead lay, exposing the remains of their deceased loved ones to the flood.

Layla knew that the woman was a stranger to the village who had arrived as a young bride from a village in Sharqia Governorate and was only willing to integrate into her new environment to a minimal extent. Layla thought the stranger had heard from her husband about the Nile flood before the High Dam was built and had perhaps wanted to imitate him by speaking of another flood, this time coming from the sky, which spared nothing in its path.

The young girl deliberately ignored the fact that the heavy rain could not be denied. When she was no longer able to ignore it, she concluded that the woman had used the rain to construct her story.

As the years went by, this memory faded away inside her and became mixed up with grandparents' stories about the Nile flood, so that the open graves appeared to her like the work of the angry river. Whenever she sat on the bank to look at the far bank, she would wonder how such a placid creation could live with a past marked by all that anger.

In al-Minya, her husband's city, Layla continued to strengthen her connection with the river. After her family connections had been severed, this taciturn, watery passageway that aroused her imagination became the sole link between her past and her present. It was true that the barriers between them had also become greater—she couldn't take off her clothes and swim in it as she did in the past, for example—but it was still her childhood friend.

2

No one is like me, as beautiful as the moon.
I am brilliant, people would walk under my light.

In her kitchen in her al-Minya apartment, Layla would sing to herself as she remembered her life far away, a childhood with which she no longer had any connection. She felt her voice was strange and distant, as if it was coming from a deep cave. She remembered the youths in the village who would stand in the street waiting for her to come out, to enjoy a glance from her on her way to draw water or to buy necessities for the house—a house that had been built of white stone at a time when all the village houses were built of unburnt bricks. The balcony had an ivy bush growing up over it, spreading its flowers over part of the roof. The courtyard was always well watered and shaded by a tall "candy apple" mulberry tree.

On one of her walks to the Nile, she was wearing an

amber necklace inherited from her grandmother. She stumbled on a stone on her way and fell on her face. Then, as she got up, the necklace got caught on a stick on the ground, the thread broke, and the beads came off. She sat crying as she collected them, then put them under the edge of her thin pink veil.

She took care to hide the beads, but her mother's watchful eyes noticed the absence of the necklace. She asked her daughter why she wasn't wearing it, and Layla stuttered and didn't reply. When her mother pressed her, she led her to the clothes cupboard, where she had hidden the small stones, wrapped in the pink veil.

Her mother's face flushed, but Layla didn't understand her mother's anger. She only knew that the simplest things could turn into a tragedy in her mother's eyes. Her mother didn't see things as other people did. Layla had heard various disconnected phrases indicating that the amber necklace was a talisman to bring luck and fertility, and that its coming undone would certainly bring some disaster.

Her mother brought some strong thread and proceeded to restring the beads. She was completely absorbed in the task as Layla watched her in confusion. What should she do? Should she leave the room to cook lunch, should she sweep the house, or stay where she was in case her mother needed something?

She always failed to anticipate what her mother would want from her, so she contented herself with staying where she was, as if she was tied up. What she chose to do was usually not what her mother wanted, and her mother would end up telling her off and complaining about her lack of judgment. But none of this could compare with her relations with her father, for her mother at least made up with her in the end and was always kind to her, even if she exaggerated her fears and warnings.

While she recognized the kinder side of her mother's personality at the time, later she was often consumed by regret whenever she thought about the stupidities of that period, when she exaggerated how different she was from her parents, her mother in particular. She started to realize that this difference was an illusion and that everyone went around an exact circle that others had gone around before in roughly the same sequence. But as soon as she felt comfortable with this idea, she recalled her son, Hisham, and rejected the idea completely. Her only son was like no one but himself. He was distant and had strange moods and habits. He was even more peculiar than his father. She blamed herself for this, firstly for her having chosen his father—with all the inconsistency and instability of his personality—as a husband, and secondly because she hadn't dealt with her son's placenta properly when it had dried and fallen out.

Her mother had often said that a baby's placenta should be left with a jeweler or in a busy market to attract wealth and prosperity, or in a mosque to bring blessing and popularity. But instead, as soon as the remaining part of Hisham's umbilical cord had become detached from his body, she had wrapped it in a kerchief and hidden it in her bra, near her heart. Then her husband appeared and they returned to the al-Minya apartment. The following day, she headed for the corniche, chose a quiet café and sat down at a table beside the Nile. Ignoring the waiter's surprise at her request, she ordered fenugreek with milk to increase the concentration of her breast milk, and while she was sipping her drink she repeated a prayer for good fortune and happiness, and threw the umbilical cord into the water. There was a strong wind, and the waves were a little stormy, so it was quickly carried away and disappeared from her sight.

She interpreted this as a sign of future prosperity, to be followed by blessings and happiness, but she later became aware of her mistake. The perpetual flow of the river from its source to its mouth made it impossible for her son to settle down happily and left him constantly confused between source and outlet; indeed, it perhaps even left him with a tendency for getting lost like his father's.

She paid her bill and got up quickly to rejoin her baby, whom she had left sleeping in the care of her neighbor, before he woke up. On her way back, she recalled that her mother had once told her that she had left her own umbilical cord in the most famous jewelers' shop in their northern province.

Whenever she recalled that detail in her old age, as she watered the pots of basil and mint on her balcony or tidied her apartment, she would repeat in a loud voice—unconcerned that someone might overhear her—that this had not improved her fortune or made her life easier, and she would immediately envision the amber beads that had become detached and mingled with the earth. The dirty amber beads were the first thing that came to her mind with any loss: a color like bees' honey, though a little darker and covered with grime, so they'd begun to resemble her monotonous life, made dusty by boredom and repetition.

She lived through the following years believing that her wretched future had been defined by that moment. Her mother's attempts to reset it on the right path by restringing the beads came to nothing. Good luck only comes once; and she—on her way to good fortune—stumbled over a personal misfortune, which from that moment did not leave her. It was the same as when she stumbled over the stranger with the sleepy look and the quiet voice at the *moulid* of al-Sayyid Badawi.

"God's blessings, Sayyid, Sheikh of the Arabs!"

"Allah, Allah, al-Badawi has brought back the prisoners!"

Every time she heard or recalled the name of al-Sayyid al-Badawi, she would chant these two phrases in a loud voice before waking up and reverting to a whisper. Then she would look at Hisham's room and confess to herself that her stumbling over the stranger in the course of the *moulid* had not been a bad thing from every point of view, if she wanted to be fair.

The *dhikr* rang out from every side as she made her way to buy the *fatira* that her mother was craving, squatting among the crowd that had come from their village to Tanta, to attend the big night at the mosque of the Ahmadiyya order, whose sheikh had been born in Fes.

The *fatira* almost fell from her hand when she bumped into him. He grabbed her to help her regain her balance, and she lifted her head to find that just a few centimeters separated his face from hers. She freed herself from his hand and stepped back without taking her eyes off his. As her heart thumped, she felt as though a fierce rain shower had fallen just on her. Then she noticed that he was in no better state than she was. But at least he was bolder—quite shameless, in fact. That is anyway what she deduced from his reaction, which made her think for a moment that he'd come across her in her village under the guava trees with her clothes off, preparing to swim in the Nile, as was her habit when there were only a few people near the river.

After this moment of doubt, she reassured herself that she was fully clothed. As she passed close to him, he didn't give her enough room to pass without touching him. Despite her embarrassment, she gave him a look of reproach with no hesitation. In the crowd, he passed his finger over the back of her hand.

It was a light, passing gesture, but it felt to her like an electric shock. She gave her mother the *fatira* and retreated into herself beside her, then clung to her, unable to calm her nerves. She didn't see him again that evening, yet she was sure he was following her from somewhere among the crowd and songs of the *mawlid*.

Secretly, she prayed that she would see him again before going back to her village the following day. She didn't realize that he had followed a reciter of the Bani Hilal epic from al-Minya, and she had no idea he'd decided to leave everything behind to catch up with her and find out everything about her and her family.

She glimpsed him passing in front of their house two days later and couldn't believe her eyes. She was hiding behind the window, looking out through a gap in the blind when she saw him loitering as he went past and staring into the house. She didn't know what she should do. Her first thought was to go out and run to him, but she was stopped by a mixture of wisdom and cowardice. With a slight shudder of her lips and a racing heart, she decided to stay where she was, or to be more precise, that there was nothing else she could do. Then she was afraid that he might despair and go back to his hometown if he didn't see her, especially since any stranger was easy to spot in a small village like hers. So she overcame her confusion and decided to go out more than usual with imaginary excuses, taking care to loiter in front of the café in the big square.

She went out five times that day in the space of two hours. When she headed for the Nile, he followed her. She was coming back with a guava she had picked from her grandfather's trees beside the river when he approached her. She stopped, not knowing what to do. She waited for him to speak, to ask her name or tell her something about himself, but all he did was to look at her for a long time. When he seemed on the verge of saying something, he changed his mind and went away, leaving her at her wits' end.

Two weeks passed without seeing him. She tried to get used to the idea that this stranger would remain a stranger and that she probably wouldn't meet him again. But eventually he did come back and ask for her hand in marriage from her father, who received him warmly and made him wait a month to make inquiries about him and his family before replying.

Before the waiting period expired, someone told her father that they had been seen together on the Nile, near the guava bushes. She swore that she had never spoken to him and didn't even know his name, but her father didn't believe her and refused to meet him. When the man came back after a month, her father told him firmly that he had no daughters available for marriage, for his daughter was engaged to her cousin. She cried and refused to eat, which only made her father more determined to not let her marry the stranger. He told the man that her cousin was more entitled to her.

To her surprise, the stranger did not disappear completely from her life but started waiting for her from time to time among the guava trees. He didn't go into the village itself but slipped from the fields on the outskirts of the village into her grandfather's orchard on the bank of the Nile.

In the thick of the almost impenetrable guava trees that were surrounded by banana groves on three sides and the Nile on the fourth, Layla discovered what she needed to know about that man from the south. There, she received her first kiss and trembled at his touches and whispers. There too, she agreed to leave with him for his city after they got married in the mosque of al-Sayyid Badawi, a few paces from the place where they had met for the first time.

More than four decades on, Layla preferred not to remember those details. She would have liked to forget them and to go back to the happy young girl she then was.

How Layla wished that the stranger had stayed a stranger!

3

Layla didn't realize where she was. She would love to get up to tidy the apartment, cook some food, and water the pots of mint and basil on her balcony, but how could she do this when she felt herself drifting like a flabby animal? No, more like a creature whose body has melted and evaporated? She recalled the amber beads that had come adrift from a necklace, which she had to bend down to pick up from the ground, wiping the earth off them and putting them in the hollow of her gown. The necklace was a bequest from her grandmother Khadija; her mother had given it to her with a request that she should leave it to her own daughter when she married and had children.

She didn't take the necklace with her when she eloped with the stranger and didn't think of it again until several years later. She thought it had never done her grandmother any good at all: it hadn't protected her from senility, or from her tendency to get lost on the paths or go crazy about them. Layla thought that if she had been able to accomplish a miracle by returning the necklace to her grandmother, perhaps everything would have returned to normal.

She felt she had become like her grandmother, a heap of bones unable to get up or walk. The difference was that the old Khadija wanted nothing more than to sit on a lambskin rug, looking at the street through a crack in the door to the last days of her life. Meanwhile, Layla scarcely knew whether she was still alive or had already traveled to another world lacking bodies, voices, or sights. All she had were the memories swimming around in her head, and ideas that went in and out of her brain with no rhyme or reason.

She missed Hisham and didn't understand where her only son had disappeared to, or how his heart had obeyed him so cruelly. She felt sorry for him. How old was he now? she wondered. In his early forties? Or mid-forties? The idea disturbed her. She had only ever looked at her son as a child needing protection and guidance—not forgetting rebuke if need be, and it was often needed, especially in regard to his absolute rejection of marriage.

Sometimes she became curious to know if her brother had married and had children. Did he have a daughter to whom the amber necklace had been passed down, or a son who knew nothing about his aunt and her son? She felt depressed, then laughed at herself, amazed that she could be bothering with these things when she didn't understand her own situation properly. Where was she? Why did she no longer feel pain? What was the cause of this feeling of floating that came over her?

There was only silence and emptiness and a darkness

that did not stop one from seeing. Or perhaps it wasn't darkness, thought Layla.

It was hard to describe what was around her. She had never been good at describing things. She had only been good at arguments and fights and blaming those who upset her with an enviable skill. But she had often proved incapable of describing love and affection. She believed that some people were born unprogrammed for expressing feelings of joy or satisfaction or love, even if they were completely surrounded by them, but experienced them alone in silence.

The feeling of floating clung to her. She would feel herself swimming in a gently rocking space as if she were being carried along on the surface of the water, as if the Nile was embracing her and carrying her on its journey toward the North. Without any flood or demons, the river reclaimed her again, not as a swimmer seeking seclusion in it in the absence of other people, but as a spirit floating on its surface, at one with it, moving with it from one village to another, in the hope that one day she might reach her birthplace.

Suddenly she was drowning in an endless lightness. Veils were ripped away that had long shaded her sight. The woman girdled in black who lived in the house next to the graveyards appeared. She was no longer glowering, but had become quite relaxed and friendly, busy with something that Layla could not make out at first until she saw they were piles of jasmine, which the woman was trying to arrange in geometrical shapes. She sat among them, fingering the delicate flowers and dividing them into smaller piles. Then she shook her hand vigorously, and the jasmine flew up in every direction. Immediately, Layla had the bright idea that a noble soul was suspended in every one of the flying flowers.

The woman disappeared just as suddenly as she had appeared, and in her place came grandmother Khadija, in the bloom of youth, before she became old and senile. She looked like a young girl, with sharp features and a knowing look, walking in a vast desert, not a breath of wind in the void, no oasis or water well in sight. Despite this, the grandmother walked without hesitation, briefly pausing from time to time to inspect her clothes at her waist, then walking on when she was reassured by their condition.

Layla saw her mother stringing the amber beads together on a thread while she sang a popular song about waiting patiently, her father sitting under the mulberry tree in the courtyard of their house reading the Qur'an, and her husband, the stranger wandering aimlessly forever intoxicated with Jabir Abu Husayn's recitation of the tale of the battle of Hasan and Diyab and Ghanim with Abu Zayd al-Hilali. Another woman approached him with a glass of dark-colored tea. As he stretched out his hand to take the glass from her and to sit her down beside him, Layla wondered who the woman could be, though she had no real wish to learn the answer.

Suddenly the Nile stretched before her as if it had expanded to encompass the whole world, and Layla recalled that she had given birth to her son, Hisham, near the river. This didn't just mean he had been born in a village or town that the mighty river flowed past; she had literally given birth to him on its banks. She was in her ninth month, forced to gather alone the okra crop that had been planted on his paternal grandfather's land. Her husband had vanished, another one of his habitual disappearances that she did not understand, and his parents asked her to stay with them in their village—which was in the Bani Mazar district—for fear that she might experience unexpected birth pangs on her own in the al-Minya apartment.

She gave in to their request reluctantly, but instead of submitting to rest in the final weeks of her pregnancy, she found herself asked to work in the fields. She didn't object, because the agricultural land next to the river, or "the sea," as she usually called it, reminded her of the place where she had been born and made her feel she had somehow returned to her family and her past.

She was bending over the okra plants to pick them, ignoring their small thorns, when she felt a sharp pain and then a stickiness between her legs. She calmed herself by saying they were passing labor pains, and she would be able to get back to her in-laws' house as soon as the pains had finished, before they came again. She figured she wouldn't give birth before midnight. She looked at the setting sun as if to seek reassurance from it, but this naturally never came.

The labor pains grew faster, and a warm liquid flowed from inside her. She could barely reach the end of the field, with the river and the willow tree whose branches dipped over the water. She clung to the soft willow branches, hiding her screams. The sun began to disappear, leaving behind it a trace of orange that colored the sky and a darkness that slowly crept onward. There was no one around as the waters of the Nile flowed silently on, suggesting that this river was a place of stillness that never knew movement.

She thought she fainted, then regained consciousness when she heard the cries of her son as he first emerged into the world. Between fainting and waking, she felt a luminous being emerge from the water to help her give birth, a feminine being with long black hair and an ethereal body that could hardly be seen. Soon afterward, her mother-in-law arrived to look for her, as she was late coming back to the house, and shouted for help when she saw Layla lying there unable to catch her breath, with her naked baby soaked in the sticky fluids of her womb, seated between her legs and screaming nonstop.

The neighbors had heard her cries for help and sent for the midwife, who cut the umbilical cord, which was later thrown into the Nile at al-Minya. Layla and her baby were then carried to her in-laws' house. For days she was haunted by an old prophecy of a wandering gypsy who read her palm when she was a child and told her that the water would swallow her children and that her grave and theirs would be submerged in it.

Layla took no notice of the woman's words at the time. The future seemed far away and children were just a distant dream, but as she was giving birth she found herself in the clutches of nightmares, overwhelmed by floods that spared nothing. When she returned to her apartment in al-Minya, after her husband had reappeared, the nightmares disappeared and the prophecy gradually vanished in the desert of oblivion.

Now Layla recalled the prophecy with the intensity of the midday sun. She thought about it as she floated gently, gliding over the surface, moving between the faces of everyone she had known in her life except for her brother and her son, who didn't appear to her, though Hisham was somehow with her. From some hidden direction, the vibrations of his unease, his sorrows, and his confusion reached her.

He was the last person she had seen in al-Minya. That day, he had been angry and melancholy, as usual over the last few years when he had come back home. He reproached her because she had forgotten to take her medicine and insisted on going with her to the doctor. Against her objections, he helped her put on her black cloak and supported her the whole way, but instead of heading for the medical office in Palace Square, he took her to sit down beside the Nile.

"A bit of fresh air and everything will be okay!"

She was happy with this change in plans. She no longer liked this square, and her spirits would drop whenever she was forced to pass through it during her periodic doctor visits. The feeling started at the time of the 2013 sit-ins and the violence that followed there. Whenever Hisham went out during that period, she was plagued by fears and nightmares until he came back.

The last time they sat together, Layla had noticed how he avoided looking at her. He was absentminded and preoccupied with something she couldn't identify or understand, especially in light of the improvement in his material circumstances beyond what she could have expected or dreamed of. She remembered how they had walked together beside the river and how she had stumbled over a rock, the hand stretched out to her and how she had grabbed it.

A light breeze was rustling the broad leaves on the banana trees on the other bank. The Nile was rough, reminding her of the angry ancient river in the tales of the ancestors. The hand was soft at first, then it turned into another hand, angry and upset. Layla took refuge in the hand, but it thrust her away instead of embracing her and holding her gently.

Then the hand disappeared, and Layla felt exhausted. As she fell down, she lost track of everything except for a sigh full of pain, an anguished voice like that of her son, and the sound of her body hitting the water. A horrendous scream pierced through her, and a limitless number of thorns penetrated her soul. As the sky fell onto the earth, she was crushed between them before tranquility overwhelmed her and her world turned to a bright whiteness. Rocked by a gently flowing stream of water, she began to feel she was floating on everything: her pains, her frustrations, her life, and her body itself.

INSIDE THE CHAGALL PAINTING

1

I remember a girl of around twenty who used to carry *The Great Interpretation of Dreams* by the Imam Muhammad ibn Sirin wherever she went. I know I am no longer that girl, and perhaps I never was. I rejected her, left her behind, abandoned her naked and shivering in the middle of some road, and went off alone stumbling over my footsteps.

I look in the mirror and am surprised to see her eyes meeting mine. Nothing else reminds me of her. My carefully sculpted face hardly resembles hers, which was slightly puffy, and the fine wrinkles around my mouth and over my brow set me even further apart from her. As for my body, girdled in newly acquired fat, it tells me, "I wish my youth could return one day!"

Only her eyes, with their faint smile even in the deepest sorrow, connect us, together with a copy of Ibn Sirin's book, which is always positioned near my bed, though some of its pages have been damaged by time and excessive use.

It is not just a book, and not just a way to interpret my obscure dreams, but also the one thread connecting me and one of the most complex ghosts of my past, by which I mean Hisham Khattab.

Perhaps I lost my connection with my old image the day he disappeared from my universe, or perhaps he disappeared the day I was no longer the person I had been before.

I don't know. There are many assumptions and more suspicions, but the moment I met him on the afternoon of that day at the start of the third millennium was one of the sweetest moments of my life. It was material fit to produce the most precious memories later.

Yes indeed, the aim of my life has always been to produce as many memories as possible. I was conducting some sort of experiment, though I was not totally immersed in it: a part of me continued to scrutinize it to see if it was pregnant with exciting memories or not! At the time I wasn't aware that, after a certain stage of life, we would not need excitement and suspense, but comfort and consolation.

The important thing is that I met Hisham for the first time in August 2001. The air was stifling in the public bus standing at the start of Tayaran Street near the intersection of Salah Salim Street. Fortunately, I had left well before the start of my appointment, for the roads were closed in expectation of the president's motorcade.

When it became clear to the passengers that there was no prospect of further passage any time soon, we started to leave the bus one after the other to walk toward Salah Salim Street.

It was a movement of despair, not of hope. I decided off the bat to escape from the prison of the Hot Metal Box. I forgot to confess that I suffer from claustrophobia, a fear of heights and dogs, and various other phobias there is no room to mention here. I walked for a considerable distance surrounded by the suppressed anger and rage of people walking beside me as they glared at the stopped cars waiting for the lights to turn, amid whispers that the motorcade had actually passed some time ago and that there was therefore no need for the delay to continue any longer.

I chose a bus stop and waited there with some other people. Among the gloomy faces I noticed his face smiling, as if he was a visitor who had chanced on this moment, or rather chanced on the whole world. His eyes were fixed on me, or to be more precise, on the book I was carrying.

"I advise you to read Freud's interpretation."

"Do you know Carl Jung?"

"Interpreters of dreams, my eyes won't sleep."

Those were the sort of comments that my constant companion on paper attracted. With Hisham, it was different. He asked me about the book with interest and wanted to know where I had bought it.

"Where did I buy it from? From the 'Ukaz market? From the sidewalk beside the al-Is'af metro station? Yes, exactly! From the old books display in front of the al-Is'af post office."

That is the reply I thought of, and which I actually repeated to myself, then thought better of it and replied, "From a bookseller at the al-Is'af station."

It was strange, nice, and refreshing to be treated by someone I had only just met for the first time with the familiarity of someone resuming a conversation with an old friend. I looked around me and found that everyone was ignoring us in the fever of waiting and expectation.

It was only a few moments before he grabbed my copy and started to thumb through it, searching for what I don't know. He reached a page, which I couldn't identify, read what was on it with great attention, then absentmindedly returned the book to me.

He talked about the August weather, the crowds, and the noise in Cairo, but his carefree expression had left him. Finally, the road was opened, and the cars raced off with a vengeance for having been detained all this time. He invited me to take a taxi with him since we were both going downtown.

"Do I know you well enough, my lad, to take a taxi with you?"

These words never escaped the prison of my mind. As usual, I kept them to myself but thanked him and made my excuses, fearing that he might form a bad impression of me if I accepted his offer. At that period, I was the prisoner of certain illusions. He asked for my phone number, but instead I told him that I regularly followed the screenings at the Cultural Cinema Center in Sharif Street.

"We'll see."

And I did see. I saw him again two months later.

I had just come out from a showing of François Truffaut's *The Green Room* when I found him smoking a cigarette outside. He said he'd come here more than once but hadn't bumped into me until now.

"I was ill for two weeks and was too lazy to come the third week."

I actually hadn't missed a screening in the two months, but I went along with his white lie. I concluded that he had deliberately been slow to come to look for me, in an attempt to set his own rules. We walked to the Filfila restaurant and ate koshari with kofta there, then headed for Zahrat al-Bustan, where we sat for two hours or more.

Once we had parted, I realized that we had hardly said anything personal to the other, even though we had talked almost nonstop. I only knew his first name, for example. I hadn't asked him for his phone number or asked if we should meet again. And he in turn hadn't asked me about anything personal. Our chitchat seemed pleasant at the time, but as soon as I returned home the details disappeared from my head.

The days turned, the days passed...

I didn't see him again for another two months. The center was screening Jean-Luc Godard's *Goodbye to Language*. He arrived in time to watch the film from the beginning and sat beside me so engrossed that he seemed to have forgotten my existence.

"God preserve you, my spirit!"

In the brief glances I snatched at him, I was astonished to see the effect of the continuous screening on his face. As we left the building, he gave me a volume of paintings by Marc Chagall. The introduction and commentary on the pictures were in Russian. He told me he had found it among the displays of old books along the wall in the Ezbekiyya, had flicked through it, and felt that the women in the pictures were like me. He chose a picture of a promenade, in which Chagall was standing in a black suit, happily holding the hand of his wife, Bella Rosenfeld Chagall, who was hovering in space above him.

He took a postcard out of his pocket with the same painting on it and gave it to me. He said I was Bella Rosenfeld.

"Okay. It doesn't matter!"

I looked at the painting but couldn't put my finger on the point of resemblance between me and the woman depicted in it. On the first page inside the cover of the volume was a dedication in green ink, in Hisham's handwriting, artistically drawn:

> To the beautiful woman who flies like Chagall's women.

"Thank you!"

We wandered around the streets downtown for some time, then he escorted me to the 'Abd al-Mun'im Riyad stop for me to board the bus to Madinat Nasr. This time, before I got on the bus, he gave me a card with his full name and phone number on it.

I looked at Bella Rosenfeld for a long time, as she appeared in Chagall's paintings or in images I found on the internet, and I was gradually persuaded that I did resemble her. I also started to share his view of her as "the most beautiful woman in the world," as he had previously described her to me. I dyed my brown hair black, like her, cut it like hers, and tried to conjure her same profound look. I wasn't trying to imitate her, for how could I imitate a woman I'd never actually seen? I wanted to become her.

Hisham never commented on these efforts of mine.

I thought he hadn't noticed them. And I had every right to think this, given that he avoided referring to the changes in my appearance, even in a passing way. Instead, he showed a strange interest in my copy of *The Great Interpretation of Dreams* by the Imam Muhammad ibn Sirin. He asked me about it, or rather interrogated me about it, repeatedly. Why did I always carry it with me? Where had I bought it from? And why was I so interested in it?

At first, I responded patiently and in detail, even as he kept repeating the same questions over and over again. Then this began to irritate me, especially as he never came back to the conversation about Chagall or Bella Rosenfeld. It also seemed unnatural for an expert on rare books, as he had described himself, to get so agitated about an ordinary copy of a book that was being sold on almost every sidewalk. I started to be evasive with him, and when he noticed this, he stopped questioning me and asked to borrow the volume. He kept it for a while, then when he returned it to me, I noticed some markings in green ink under certain lines, and comments, most of which I didn't understand, in the margins of the pages, with repeated drawings of flowers that looked like jasmine next to them.

I didn't comment on his scrawls and scribbles in my book, but I did look at them from time to time. I felt they were drowning me in a world whose outline I could not distinguish but which in some obscure way was leading me astray. I looked at the drawings and the scribbles and saw palm groves and vines surrounded by jasmine shrubs, the green of which was almost hidden behind the white of the flowers. Then the flowers began to drop until they covered the ground of the orchard, before everything disappeared and I saw the page of the book with the underlinings and the hazy drawings in the margins.

The book itself no longer held the same attraction for me as Hisham's vague scribblings. I liked the idea of getting to know him through what he wrote in the margins of his own books, so I asked him to lend me some books from his library. I was disappointed to find them empty of any writing or drawings, or even a simple fold here and there. With the exception of his name, which was written on the first inside page of every book, they were all as if they had just come off the press. Even the comments written on the old volumes were in handwriting completely different from his own perfectly executed script.

I advised him to read *The English Patient* and gave him my own copy. When he returned it to me some time later, I opened it impatiently but didn't find any sign that his pen had passed over it. If he hadn't discussed the events and characters with me, I would have thought he hadn't touched it.

Until that moment, I hadn't found out anything about him to satisfy my curiosity. His interest in me was plain from his looks and actions, but he didn't let a single word escape from him to acknowledge or define this interest. The hidden part of my relationship with him was several times greater than the open part, though this did not disturb me at the time. I comforted myself with the thought that it was a matter of time, nothing more, and waited for him to confess his love for me sooner or later. But then he disappeared from my world for a time.

"The absent one always has an excuse."

I waited for him every time I returned to the Cultural Cinema Center. When he finally appeared, he told me his father had died and that he had to travel to al-Minya to console his mother and receive the mourners. He explained they had had no news of their father for several years and news of his death in Libya had only just reached them. He spoke with indifference, which I attributed to the father's absence from his life for several years. When I went up to him and embraced him, he seemed confused and looked around us, then embraced me in return. At that moment, I knew that a barrier that had separated us had fallen away, and we started to meet almost every day. I would leave the gallery where I worked to meet him in a café downtown, then we would choose somewhere to eat, then wander around until he escorted me to the 'Abd al-Mun'im Riyad stop for me to catch the bus home. But instead of all this strengthening the bond between us, I started to notice his distance from me, and how he was slipping through my fingers.

There was plenty of water under the bridge in our relationship when he shocked me—sitting in a crowded café in a narrow alley joining Mahmoud Bassiouney and Kasr El-Nil Streets—with the news that he wouldn't be able to leave his mother to live alone in the state she was in. He didn't explain what he meant by "the state she was in," and I thought he would just live with her temporarily until her situation improved and then come back to live in Cairo. Once I realized what he meant, all my subsequent efforts to persuade him not to move to al-Minya failed. I didn't realize that my contact with him would be confined to phone conversations he would generously grant me from time to time, and never once would he suggest there was anything special drawing us together. In response, I replied cursorily to his questions in the hope that it would discourage him from continuing to contact me.

"If you want us to go back as we were, tell time to go back, time!"

The gaps between the telephone calls grew longer and the periods of silence during them more drawn out. He seemed to be trying to find words with which to draw out the thread of our conversation, while I took pleasure in his confusion. I didn't understand his insistence on having these wretched conversations when he had abandoned me like someone avoiding the plague.

Until a day came when I met him by chance on 26 July Street—near the junction with Talaat Harb Street, to be precise. I couldn't help feeling annoyed that he hadn't told me he would be in Cairo, but despite that I said hello, and he returned the greeting with interest, though he seemed distant and preoccupied. I invited him for a coffee in the Shams café nearby, and he accepted without enthusiasm, insisting on paying himself.

He confessed that he visited Cairo from time to time for reasons connected with his work. His politeness was exaggerated and I noticed that he avoided looking me directly in the eye, though I didn't understand why. He left after less than an hour. He didn't call me, and I didn't try to contact him for years afterward.

As time went on, I became certain that, however you described what was between us, it was not love. At the end of our relationship, I thought I had lost him at some crossroads, for a reason that I didn't properly comprehend, and now I doubt if I ever really won him.

When I remember him, the words of Najat's song reverberate in my mind: "I was still in love, still learning anew. I didn't know that close to you was far away."

I start to sing, and laugh, grateful to time for the blessing of forgetfulness.

2

Is there something called "sand phobia"? If it existed, it is certain I would suffer from it.

Bravo!

A new phobia to be added with pride to my phobia assortment. I never thought before that my hatred of those soft yellow grains could be pathological, but the idea has some validity, and my feelings toward it are violent enough to keep me awake, exactly like my feelings toward any phobia I suffer from.

Sand has never stopped disturbing me. Just seeing it leaves a bitter taste inside me, a taste of sadness and regret, which brings on trembling and a stomachache. On the few occasions when my family went for a vacation at Ras al-Barr or Marsa Matruh, I would stay in the sea for as long as possible, playing with my brothers and clinging to my father, while my mother followed us from where she was sitting on the beach.

I hated the moment when I would be forced to step onto the sand in my bare feet. I never played in it like the other children. I never built sandcastles, which would be quickly swept away by a wave, and I never dug holes to fill up with a small plastic bucket. I used to sit on my own special chair, my legs folded underneath me, trying to forget that the sand had just touched them.

I would shut my eyes, and in my mind's eye I would see a scene of spiders invading a dusty house and scorpions making their way through the desert.

"Too many phobias, people! A cocktail to refresh the spirits! Come on, over here!"

"Arachnophobia, scorpiophobia, desertophobia!"

Now I live in al-'Ubur city, where the surrounding sprawl reminds me of the desert and conjures up a mental image of continuous sand. I try to convince myself that I am lucky to have escaped the crowds and hubbub of Cairo, but deep down I long for them in every detail, or to be more precise, I long for my carefree childhood and youth I spent there and hanker after my dreams of beginnings, some of which I have given up while others have proved too difficult.

As soon as I graduated, I tried to work in journalism, but all the doors were shut in my face. I wrote a report about film-poster workshop artists for a magazine and was alarmed to find it published under someone else's name. When I complained, I was given eighty Egyptian pounds, which was less than I had spent in the course of preparing the report. After that, I knocked (to no avail) on the doors of several Arabic magazines and newspaper offices in Cairo, until a staff member in one of them took pity on me, took me aside, and advised me to spare myself the trouble, unless I had some powerful connections.

"Don't waste your time, my girl, if you don't have *wasta!*"

Through a friend I had gotten to know through my regular attendance at the Cultural Cinema Center's screenings and various cultural clubs, I found work at a gallery in Zamalek. It was a nice job that gave me many contacts, and through it I learned a lot about fine arts.

It was during this period that I met Hisham Khattab. He didn't ask me what I did for a living at first and grew interested when I subsequently told him the name of the gallery where I worked: Chagall. When I told him of my aborted dream to work in journalism and of my report that had been attributed to someone else, he gave an enigmatic smile and said, "It's normal, it happens!"

His reactions were unpredictible. He laughed at tragic things and got angry at trivial matters, while he might not object to crimes committed against himself.

As our relationship grew stronger, he told me that attributing our work to others was something that happened on a daily basis. I didn't understand what he meant at first, until he explained that he worked with a well-known researcher and writer, helping him to collect research materials and writing comments and notes on them, and this man would often include these comments in his books and paper just as they were, without indicating who had written them.

When I angrily asked him how he could not object to something like this, he shrugged his shoulders in a disinterested way, made no comment, and avoided broaching the subject again. He seldom alluded to the person he called "my professor," and if he did, it would be in a different context.

Hisham's entry into my life was gentle and gradual. He penetrated every aspect of it calmly, without even realizing it.

"Welcome! Your house and your place!"

All my actions implicitly told him this, but he remained hesitant, taking one step forward and several steps back. He would speak quite openly and reveal the deepest secrets of his childhood and youth, his ambitions and fears, then raise his invisible armor as a barrier between us again. Every time he talked uninhibitedly about himself, I expected a subsequent period of retreat on his part, or at least a period of reticence in which he would turn into a hedgehog sticking its spines into my face. He would become hurtful with his harsh replies, sudden bursts of anger, and cruel silence about wrongs I could not define but could only guess at from the accusing looks he shot at me. Eventually, he decided to run away, with an abandon that startled me, even though my pride prevented me from showing my disappointment.

I was never convinced by his declared reasons. Of course, I understood that his father had died a few months before, but he had spent this period in Cairo and not thought to return to stay with his mother at once. I think that the idea never occurred to him until after the fire, which happened three weeks before he decided to leave Cairo. During this period, he seemed distracted and evasive. I initially attributed this to sadness, and was surprised that he seemed more upset than he was when his father had died.

I distrusted my intuition and knowledge of his personality for four years, for the Hisham I knew didn't care about death and disasters so much as I sometimes felt he had been born without a single atom of empathy. He used to deal with everything with a stoicism I could never accept. The only time I saw him respond visibly to an external event occurred during the invasion of Iraq.

During that period, he followed developing events as though his life depended on their outcome. I was with him when he learned that the British had occupied Basra, and I saw the impact the news had on him. He cried and collapsed, banging his head on the wall. He didn't talk about politics in front of me, and seldom commented on any general development, so I was extremely surprised by his reaction, especially as he remained affected for a long time afterward. He let his beard grow and neglected his appearance as a chasm began to open up between him and his personality as I had known it. He became extremely withdrawn and secretive, as well as aggressive, unable to stand any criticism of his actions. He would take pleasure in my tears and suffering, accusing me of playing the victim, and he started to call me "the martyr." Then, when the news came of his father's death, followed some months later by the fire, he surprised me with his determination to go back to stay in al-Minya.

Despite all my reservations about his life changes, I was sorry that he had excluded me from his calculations for the future. I didn't know how to behave, or how to prevent him from proceeding with his plans. I told him impetuously that I was expecting his child. We were sitting in a café, whose name I don't recall, in a covered corridor between Mahmoud

Bassiouney Street and Kasr El-Nil Street downtown when he leapt to his feet. He seemed about to say something, but instead he turned and fled without a word, as if trying to outrun the plague. The customers in the café stared at me curiously for a few moments, then went back to their gossip and backgammon. I tried to conceal my embarrassment and pretended to hunt for something in my handbag. I didn't understand what had come over me to make me invent this lie, but the devil whispered in my ear that I could not retreat from it.

Hisham disappeared for two days, then called me on the third day, asking to meet so we could look for a solution to the problem.

"What problem?"

"Stop being stupid!"

Even though, at that moment, I would have liked him to leave the world, not just Cairo, and not come back, I agreed to meet him in the Phoenix Café on Emad El-Din Street in two hours' time. I was deliberately late, and when I arrived, he was extremely tense. He told me his circumstances would not allow him to form a relationship with me or anyone else and that I would have to have an abortion. He would give me the necessary money and the address of a doctor who was specialized in these matters.

A classic film scene, done to death by the black-and-white films. I had only myself to blame. I brought it on myself.

At first I said nothing. I finished my coffee slowly, then picked up my bag to leave. I didn't look behind me to see what effect my actions had had on him. I consoled myself that I was lucky to have discovered his true personality, instead of retaining it in my memory in its radiant form. But as the years passed, his negative aspects slipped away and only his positive qualities were preserved in my memory. What remained was the gentle person I had met the first time, had gradually become attracted to, and whose name had become synonymous with my days of freedom and liberation.

After that, I saw him twice—or perhaps it was once for real and once in my imagination. The first time, we met by chance on 26 July Street on one of his visits to Cairo. I invited him for a coffee in the Shams café. It was a meeting framed by hesitation and embarrassment. The second time, I noticed him in the distance in Tahrir Square, the day Mubarak relinquished power. About seven years had passed since he moved to al-Minya, and I had never expected to see him in the square. I didn't approach him, and as soon as I noticed him, he was swallowed up by the crowds with no warning, so I persuaded myself that I had merely imagined seeing him.

Two years after that day, I was surprised to receive a Friend request from him on Facebook. My first reaction was to reject it, to prevent him approaching my world, even if only virtually, but I was too curious not to accept his request. Sometimes I looked at his image, trying to trace the effects of time on the face I had once known so well. All I could notice, apart from a few white hairs that had crept across his head and some light wrinkles around his eyes, was that his look had acquired a severity that had not been so pronounced before, and that his face had taken on a new sternness.

Most of what he wrote about was quite obscure to me, things like talismans and charms that no one but he would understand. Even when he wrote about current events, his words seemed ludicrously complicated. From time to time, he would comment on a picture of mine or a post that I had shared on my page. I would be annoyed for a bit afterward, because his comments were usually ambiguous, and because of my growing ill will toward him, I would interpret his words in the most negative way possible.

As time went on, I no longer cared what he wrote, as I was aware that most of it was stamped with the madness of insecurity and persecution, together with an exaggerated estimation of himself. The worse the general situation became, the more detached from reality he appeared, and his posts acquired a hallucinatory, mystical gloss that I had not noticed in him before.

He started to claim that he had a solution to all the problems of the country and that he had prepared files to clarify his program for solving the expected water crisis, as well as inflation and power shortages, and just wanted someone to help him reach the president to explain it all to him.

At the time, I used to tell myself, "Leave creation to the Creator, and just enjoy the show," ignoring the fact that current economic and political circumstances left no room for enjoyment in our lives. I only stopped being a spectator when he took a picture of my child and made it his "profile image." I wrote to him angrily and demanded that he change the picture, at which point he started sending me rude messages accusing me of deserting and abandoning him.

"No, sir!!!"

He started to pursue me with affected, syrupy phrases, misrepresenting the details of our relationship and absolving him of all wrongdoing. At first I couldn't be bothered to reply to them, then I could no longer find sufficient energy to read them at all. Every morning there would be a new message from him, as if my refusal to reply or even to open his messages hadn't bothered him in the least.

The strange thing is that I didn't feel any satisfaction when his messages stopped and he disappeared from Facebook. His account wasn't closed, he just stopped updating it. I very much wanted to know why he had vanished. My curiosity began like a small seed that I tried to bury inside me, but from it sprang a tree whose branches grew to fill my whole being and drove me to imagine possible scenarios for the direction his life had taken since we had parted. But my imagination usually failed me, leaving me to daydream of an alternative life in which we were joined together and had raised a small family before our relationship drowned in monotony and annoyance. This was a great consolation to me. It was true that I was living alone with my child after her father had died, but my life certainly wasn't boring. My existence was divided between looking after my child and running the clothes "boutique" I had inherited from my late husband.

3

Hisham lived in his own private world. He spoke with confidence about how he would do this or that in a certain number of years, regardless of whether he had the necessary abilities to accomplish these goals. His relationship with money was complicated; sometimes he would act as if he didn't care about it, while at other times it seemed that wealth was his sole objective and the route that led to all his dreams.

He could be generous to the point of extravagance or careful to the point of miserliness. But with the exception of his fondness for splendid houses, he was not attached to luxuries, and for a long time he preferred to frequent simple, inexpensive cafés and restaurants, even when he had a large income. The one time we went to the Tavern restaurant and bar, in the Nile Hilton hotel, he was tense and nervous the whole time. He ordered an excessive quantity of expensive food and drinks and gave the waiter a large tip. Then he started acting strangely, looking around nervously, before dragging me outside. He only regained his composure when we reached Talaat Harb Square. In the streets downtown, he used to move like someone walking around his own house.

We would sit in a sidewalk café or in a narrow corridor between two buildings, where he would occupy himself with a crossword. He would finish it in record time, remember that I was with him, and direct a question or remark to me quite unconnected to anything. At which point, I would figure that his mind must have wandered, perhaps to some other place or maybe some other time, and that he had said the first thing that occurred to him, just to reassure me that he was aware of my presence beside him and was open to talking with me.

What I never understood was his habit of reading the classified advertisements every day. Focusing on luxury properties, he would write down anything that caught his attention in a special notebook, then call the number provided to find out as much as he could about the property in question. If feasible, he would go to see it, posing as a prospective buyer with the means to purchase it. In these circumstances, he would be at his most sparkling, discussing the details seriously, wandering around the apartment or villa, examining the rooms and windows and sources of light, and asking about anything that caught his attention. He was so believable in this guise that on the few occasions when I accompanied him on these ludicrous missions, I thought he actually did have the means to purchase something that splendid and expensive, so good was he at playing the part of the rich purchaser.

Hisham became angry when I asked him why he didn't try his luck at acting. He said he wasn't acting; he just liked to listen to what these exquisitely tasteful houses said to him, and that one day he would purchase one of them.

Things went smoothly when the person responsible for our tour of the apartment was the agent, not the owner. Even if the agent had doubts about the financial capacity of the presumed client, he would continue his work in a professional, routine way. When the owners were involved, Hisham would sometimes become flustered if he said something wrong and felt his appearance and person being scrutinized more carefully as a result.

My worst experience with him in this respect happened when we went to view a duplex apartment at the Ard al-Golf neighborhood in Heliopolis. The advertisement made the apartment look magnificent and enormous, but as soon as the owner opened the door and looked at us, he told us the apartment had already been sold. This was despite Hisham having called him an hour previously to confirm the appointment. The man shut the door hard in our faces, and the whole way from Heliopolis to downtown, I was conscious of Hisham seething beside me. He didn't say anything, but I was certain he was feeling badly insulted. He decided we should go back by tram that day. We sat with our backs to the direction of travel, facing the spot we had started from. We didn't exchange a single word, and I avoided looking at him. Despite my vow not to get drawn into his fantasies in the future, I found myself joining him two weeks later in a similar adventure, this time to see a luxury apartment in the Maryoutiya district, on the top floor of a two-story villa.

The person who met us had left us to inspect the apartment at our leisure after giving us some basic information about the place and retreating to the ground floor.

This was the first time I had seen bedrooms each equipped with a private bathroom. I especially liked the bathroom off the main bedroom, with its dark pink porcelain and circular bath. It looked to me like a play area. I understood then what Hisham meant when he said that houses divulged their secrets to him. I felt this luxury apartment had something to tell me. I wanted it for my own home, and Hisham noticed that.

We spent a long time examining it. We stood in front of every window and gazed at the view from its enormous balcony. I told Hisham that the tree overlooked by the master bedroom was called a bombax, and its orange flowers were almost the color of carrots. He nodded in agreement and pointed to another tree of the same species with bright flowers, facing the balcony, then had a good laugh at the tree's name.

In the opposite direction stood a mango grove, with part of a school playground beside it. We knew from the ad that it was the Japanese School in Cairo. Hisham gently pressed my hand and seemed to get lost in the scene in front of us.

As we were leaving, Hisham told me this apartment would bring us together one day, and I believed him. His words seemed more like a promise than a wish.

His material circumstances had begun to improve at the time, and I recall asking him if his professor had raised his salary. He replied that he hardly received a penny from helping the man and that his main source of income was his work in the antique book and rare print trade.

"Then why do you work with him?"

He shook his head and gave a vague laugh without replying to my question.

Despite the enjoyment I took from looking at this apartment with him and my pleasure when he said it would bring us together, I stopped accompanying him on this sort of expedition after that. I went back to my family home that day to look at every detail of it with a critical, angry eye. It looked untidy, old and too small. I was also afraid of dreaming about something that was difficult or even impossible to achieve.

I was right, for after a short period, Hisham's treatment of me began to change. His hostility and his criticism intensified, as did the way he made fun of me. He seemed wrapped up in himself, behaving like a frightened, rolled up hedgehog, ready to poke its spines in my face at the slightest slip on my part.

"It could have been worse. I don't care about this person anymore! At least he prepared me psychologically for being abandoned."

I remember now that before he stopped updating his Facebook account, he posted some pictures that I recognized as the view from the Maryoutiya villa. Of course, I'm not certain they were the same pictures, so many years after our only visit there, but the view corresponded with my recollections of it: a bombax tree with orange flowers, mango trees in the distance, and most important, the window frame with its tastefully worked woodwork, impossible to forget.

I didn't understand what message Hisham wanted to

convey by these pictures. I was sure they were a message directed at me in particular and nobody else. Two days later, he posted a selfie of him with a young woman with short black hair and strong features. They were standing on a balcony like the one in the Maryoutiya villa, with the bombax branches behind them, against a background of the mango grove. The woman looked happy, unconcerned by the breeze playing with her hair, which was flying left and right. As for Hisham, the expression on his face was gloomy, and his eyes had the look of loneliness and death.

After a few hours, Hisham took the picture down, leaving me to wonder about the identity of his companion, anxious to know what had happened to him in the years that followed his disappearance from the horizon of my own life and changed him into this misrepresentation of himself. The dejection settled over his pale face frightened me. My fear had its origins in the games played by fate. If any of us could see as a child how they would look in middle or old age, they would be terrified.

I think about this as I look at myself in my bedroom mirror, in the hope of finding on my tired face a glimpse of the remains of my youth that have slipped through my fingers.

A WOMAN IN AL-KARKH: A HOUSE ON THE OUTSKIRTS OF BASRA

I

During a visit to al-Karkh for something or other, I by chance met Mujiba, decades after we had last seen each other. It was a misty morning, and I was preoccupied with the memory of Yazid ibn Abihi. I had been thinking about him since earlier that morning, when I noticed an old woman selling pears in the market. She was wearing poor, rough clothes, and only her hands and face were visible.

Something about her seemed familiar. I looked into her eyes closely and despite the lines around them and her pallid look, I recognized that they were the eyes of Mujiba. I trembled, for the old woman in front of me looked like she had just risen from the dead.

As I told her that I wanted to buy all her goods, on the condition that she helped me carry them home, she hardly looked at me. I gave her more than the price she was asking, and she carried the pears with me, stumbling as she walked, for time had not been kind to her. She followed me to a house I had bought especially for my visits to Baghdad.

She put her goods down in the garden of the house and refused to go any further. I called her by her name and asked her how she was. She didn't seem surprised, nor did she pretend not to remember me. Instead, she just looked at my fine clothes and the opulent-looking house without comment.

I insisted that she come in for a short rest and sent the servant to bring her food and drink from the market. I told her all I wanted from her was to know all that had happened to her since she left Basra.

She ate the meat and pomegranate stew, broth, and honey sweets the servant brought in with the appetite of someone who hadn't tasted food for years. She told me what she had lived through. Her voice was dry and distant, and her eyes had a look of reproach as if it was I who had caused all of her suffering and misfortune.

I learned from her that she had stayed in the Samawa desert for years, looking after a sick old woman and living with her in her tent before inheriting the tent after the old woman's death. She ended up marrying someone several years older than herself when she grew tired of loneliness, then moved with him from the desert to Baghdad a short time after the caliph al-Mansour had built the city. Her journey to the "City of Peace" was easier than her flight from Basra, for she and her husband traveled with a caravan of people she had lived among for a long time. They were on a visit to Baghdad for trade purposes, while she wanted to stay in the new capital for the rest of her life. She had told her husband of her comfortable circumstances to persuade him to travel with her.

They told their fellow travelers that they would stay with some relatives of hers until they could rent a house of their own. She was confident that everything would be okay so long as her bag stayed strapped to her waist. In Baghdad, after she had left the caravan, she didn't know where to begin or where she could stay, but her husband took her to a khan and rented a room for the two of them, telling her that he would look for a small house to stay in temporarily.

She had already told him she had inherited the jewels and gold coins from her first husband and tried to persuade him to buy an enormous house and live a life of luxury, but he insisted on making do with a small house so that the money would not run out too quickly.

She admired his sound judgment when he told her that it would be better to use any remaining money for commerce, so that it would accumulate rather than be frittered away over time through overspending.

As soon as they had settled in the new house, her husband started to stay away most of the day, on the pretext that he wanted to get to know the city merchants and markets in order to decide which trade would be most suitable for the pair of them. One morning, she woke up and was shocked to find that he had disappeared with the contents of the bag, apart from a handful of coins he had left her so she wouldn't die of hunger.

I sought God's protection from abandonment after virtue, as I heard her add that she hadn't known what to do.

She regretted entrusting him with her money, though she had been forced to do so to persuade him to accompany her to Baghdad. She didn't want to repeat her mistake when she fled from Basra with no protection and no companion. Now she was in Baghdad, but the city, which was full of people and markets, had been shut in her face. Here she was a weak, unaccompanied woman, with only a small amount of money left.

After the howling and crying and imploring the man to return the money, she realized that her hopes and journey had ended here. She thanked God that she had a roof over her head to save her from vagrancy and tried to think of an occupation that would spare her poverty. But all she could find to do was to sell in the markets, while she kept herself alive on coarse *khushkar* bread and oil, with some roots and herbs supplied by the earth.

I was disturbed by this story of the bag of jewels and gold coins and did not believe Mujiba at first when she swore she had found them in the house she shared with Yazid in Basra and that he was hiding them behind the clothes trunk, thinking she wouldn't be able to move the heavy chest.

Yazid, as I knew, hardly paid any attention to money. The treasures of the earth could not tempt him to stray from the righteous path. On the other hand, this issue of the jewels gave some logic to Mujiba's story and the way she had fled.

My suspicions reached a peak when she told me of a sick old man whom Yazid had vaguely written about in his notes, who she had concluded must be the owner of the treasure.

I asked her to explain more about the man, and she assured me that she had understood nothing of what had been written about him. Everything relating to him in Yazid's writings, which she read surreptitiously, appeared to be the gibberish of a feverish person seeking forgiveness and expiation for an unspecified crime.

We did not mention our relationship, nor did we allude to it, either directly or indirectly. However, I did notice that she avoided mentioning my name. At the sort of age we were now, we seemed like two different people, with no connection to the past. Time was a wall dividing us from what was past, an unseen but strong and powerful barrier that could only fleetingly be penetrated to return us to our previous life through a memory that played with us according to its whims.

I gave her a sum of money to spare her the humiliation of asking and asked my servant to escort her home. I sent her away, hoping not to see her again and thinking that stranger and more curious than anything else was how God could alter men's hearts and time changed their passions. Following her disappearance, I was overcome by a fatal desire for her and wanted nothing more than to see her again and to reassure myself that she was alive and well. She held my life in her hands, and when I saw her, after all these developments, I saw someone who had dealt me a mortal blow and a violent death. And I understood the kingdom of death. Her lined face brought back the memory of how I had attacked Yazid ibn Abihi to assassinate him and buried him with my two hands, and it perpetuated my treachery and betrayal of him.

I was disturbed by the story of the sheikh that Mujiba had brought up, and hated my arrogance, which had led me to believe that Yazid was an open book to me; Malik the copyist, his companion, interpreter of his dreams, and his murderer. I stayed in Baghdad for no more than a day after that, and I never went back again.

I didn't want to be joined in a single city with Mujiba. Who could want something to remind him of the pleasure of a time whose passion has vanished but whose pain remains? Still, I would sometimes send my servant from Basra to Baghdad with some money for her. I vowed to support her so long as I was alive, and I considered this a final debt to be repaid to Yazid ibn Abihi, who had stuck with me ever since I felled him, and whose ghost I could almost see whenever I took refuge in my old hut and looked out the window toward where the jasmine had been.

Early one morning, a little before daybreak, I could almost see him wandering aimlessly, looking toward the nearby vineyard I had purchased so no one could disturb the peace of my seclusion or Yazid's final rest, or bend down to pick up the jasmine that had fallen under the tree, to inspect it and scatter it over his head, watching it as it fell.

I rub my eyes and take refuge with God from Satan the accursed. The ghost disappears from sight, but his presence in my soul grows denser. I like the idea that the whole of Yazid's life is the shadow of a ghost who had not completed his visit before announcing his departure.

When one day my servant, returning from one of his visits to Baghdad, told me that Mujiba had departed this life, I wanted my stay on this earth to end in turn. I wasn't sure whether God had forgiven my sin or not, but I no longer wanted anything more. My feeling was, as the poet Zuhair ibn Abi Sulma said:

I am tired of the cares of life, but if someone lives for eighty years, it is hardly surprising that he should be tired.

2

At a time when the plague was carrying off souls in great numbers in Basra, I, Yazid ibn Abihi, the Basran palm leaf weaver, stood in front of a house that looked rich and luxurious, with a flourishing garden in which palm trees competed with vines, citrus fruit with pears, willows with basil and jasmine, and roses with narcissi.

It looked to me like a shady paradise in the hell of my city, which was suffering from a plague from which there was no escape. I was too cowardly to visit the sick Wasil ibn 'Ata', who was isolated in his house. But I did not hesitate to creep under cover of night to the sanctuary of this mysterious house. I didn't understand how I hadn't been aware of it before, despite knowing every inch of my city as a man knows the lines on his hand.

Hearing no sound from inside, I was encouraged to continue what I had begun. The smells of the flowers and plants in the garden mingled in the silence of the night, wrapping my entire being in a fragrant cloud that kept the shadow of death and disease far from me. I looked at the sky, and the full moon gazed down at me, as if bearing witness to my being. I ignored it and tiptoed along, clutching the edges of my dress to my body so it did not rustle.

At first, I thought the house was actually empty. It looked as though the people living there had left quickly, taking the least number of possessions with them—things that were both valuable and easy to carry. Carpets were scattered here and there, and silks had been thrown on the floor.

This sight encouraged me to search through each of the rooms, one after the other. They were all empty. Then I heard a moan coming from somewhere deep inside the house. I followed the sound in trepidation, searching in my mind for a response if someone were to suddenly appear and ask me what was I doing in a house that was not mine, and to which I had not been invited.

I decided that I would say that the sound of the moaning had prompted me to go inside to see what was the matter with the person who had cried out and if they needed help. A weak excuse in this time of widespread death, but it was all my brain could come up with.

I followed the sound of moaning into a room where an old man was lying in bed, struggling to hold on to the last manifestations of life with one hand, while the other clutched a small, decorated box. Something came over me when I saw it; I was torn between several emotions.

He didn't notice me. His eyes were open, but it did not seem as if they could see anything. There was a damp cloth over his brow, and his lips were moving, saying something I couldn't understand.

I saw in the man the murky face of death, the weakness of man and his incapacity to change what had been fated for him. My devil whispered to me that I should be the master of my destiny and not wait for the blind hand of fate to play with me, that I should choose what I had to do and which road to follow.

These thoughts scared me. I sat on the edge of the bed watching the old man in his final struggle for life, resolved to intervene if necessary. I don't know how much time passed between my entering his bedroom and grabbing the cloth, which still retained some of the moisture from his brow.

I carefully placed it over his mouth and nose and stopped his last breath. His body shuddered, seeking some last gasps of life, but I did not relax my grip. Even after the spirit had left him and the hand clasping the little box had fallen away from it, I continued to hold the cloth over his face.

I was shuddering and wanted to just start screaming, but I was too scared even to whisper. I didn't know what to do with myself or with an old man who had become a lifeless corpse. I spread out the cloth and hid the box inside it, wrapped it up, and without thinking carried it away with me.

In front of the house, I looked at the sky but did not find the moon. It was hidden I knew not where, and the darkness had grown deeper. It occurred to me that by embarking on what I had done, I had hidden the celestial body and dragged darkness into the world, my world, at least.

I longed for the songs of the girls in our alley when I was

small, when there was no moon. They would sing at it to come back, while their mothers begged God for the eclipse to finish. I myself felt that the eclipse suited me perfectly. I didn't want the light of the moon to expose me to anyone's eye, despite my certainty that no one would bother with me or my victim in this time of collective death, even if they had witnessed me murdering him.

I wasn't worried as I entered my house, for Mujiba used to visit her sick mother and stay with her for two days. I had the idea that the old man had perhaps been sick with the plague, and that by going into his house and touching him I might have caught his illness and not just taken his soul, but I did not care. At the very least, I would have chosen my destiny and my path consciously, rather than falling victim to the so-called hand of fate.

I spent that night in a fever, but I didn't feel ill at all in the days that followed. I simply felt exhausted, as if I had snatched my own soul from my body, not the soul of the sick old man. In the end I opened the box, to find the jewels and gold dinars there. Only then did I hate myself. I had never wanted or chased money. My desire is for knowledge, not money or power. I have often sought refuge with the Almighty, the All-High One, from the temptation of praise, from the temptation of women, and from the temptation of hypocrisy, praying to Him that I should not be numbered among those who know only the superficial aspects of things, but rather among those who know the mysterious aspects of conduct and those things that are hidden.

As I tried to overcome my sorrow, I wrapped the jewels and dinars in the cloth and hid the bundle in a chink in the wall behind our clothes chest until I could decide what to do with it. And I hid the empty small box in my cloak, determined to rid myself of it.

At first, I thought of throwing it into the marshes, then decided that to bury it would be the ideal solution. I also knew where I would bury it. I left it in my shop and passed by Malik the copyist in the market, who told me that he would be busy until noon. So I went back to the shop and collected the empty small box, hid it in my cloak, and headed for the reed hut that belonged to the copyists. In the area in front of the shop, near the vineyard next to it, I dug up the earth and buried the box, then heaped the earth over it and leveled the spot with my feet. Then I scattered some grass and dry tree leaves over it so that it blended in with its surroundings.

I went back home, not to the market, and fell into a sleep as deep as a coma. Unusually, dreams abandoned me. They had deserted me after my crime, and while these dreams and visions used to oppress me, especially when they came true, their absence was several times more oppressive. It was a sign that I had strayed from the straight path. My fictitious excuse that I had helped the decrepit old man and given him rest from his suffering did not seem persuasive in my eyes. My doubts, and my moment of disbelief, appeared before me, and stopped me seeing anything else.

When I subsequently learned that Abu Hudhayfa al-Ghazzal had died on the same night, and perhaps at the same moment as I was smothering the old man, I felt that I was also responsible for the death of my sheikh and imam.

I remembered my old dream, which sheikh al-Hasan al-Basri had explained as the departure of the ulema of

Basra, and felt that it did not stop with this interpretation. I thought that the dream had some sort of connection with what had happened in the house on the outskirts of Basra, and with the jasmine tree in the garden and its scent, which mingled with that of other flowers. Suddenly this scent seemed to me to be the scent and harbinger of death. You were right, Hasan, my master: the first syllable of *yasmin* in Arabic means "despair."

The plague cloud left my Basra's sky, but the cloud of my crime did not leave my sky. I kept the jewels and gold dinars to remind me of what my hands had perpetrated. I thought of donating them to the needy, but I was afraid of arousing suspicion as to how I, a poor, ascetic weaver of palm leaves, had acquired precious stones and gold dinars.

As the deadly plague abated, life returned to normal and it was no longer easy to get away with such a crime, but my fear of the Lord and the torments of hell was what robbed me of my sleep. I turned in sincere repentance to the Lord of the Worlds and strove hard in my devotions and *dhikr*. I said, I will consider the return of my dreams to their previous state to be a sign that God, may He be praised and exalted, has accepted my repentance—though this sign has not yet illumined my world.

Meanwhile, Malik ibn 'Udayy the copyist was asking me about my dreams, irritated that I had stopped telling them to him and impatiently awaiting his chance to interpret them. I didn't want him to suspect anything, so I started making up dreams. Some of them were modifications of old dreams I hadn't related to him before, as I was certain that they were simply mixed-up bits and pieces with no connection whatsoever to genuine visions. Others that I made up were composed of fragments of things I had experienced during my day, blended with some fantasies of my imagination.

To my surprise, the ruse worked with the copyist, despite his intelligence. He went along with my inventions with his usual seriousness and tried hard to penetrate their mysteries.

With time, I started to notice unusual changes in him; it was as though he was avoiding looking at me and ignoring me even as he talked to me. Sometimes he was keen to stay with me all the time and would come to ask me about my plans for the day, then at other times he would simply disappear.

While I could sometimes see suffering and misery in his eyes, I often felt he was behaving as if he had just tasted the signs of paradise. I secretly wondered what he saw in my eyes when he stared into them. Would he be able to probe the depths of my hidden secrets, given his ability to discern obscure faults and precise virtues?

I praised the Lord, may he be praised and exalted, several times for the fact that the copyist had finally stopped looking in my eyes when he spoke to me, as he used to do in days gone by.

I had often believed in his ability to probe the depths of other people and get to know their innermost secrets and hidden desires. Even so, I comforted myself that God almighty would not reveal my secrets to him. Then I would again remember that everything had its time and that the time for exposing my own situation was inevitably coming.

BEHIND THE MIST OF THE BODY

I

In my head, memories awoke from their slumber, and it was no longer possible to suppress them. I say that they were my own memories, the memories of Hisham Khattab, in a previous existence, while they told me that they were the memories of Yazid ibn Abihi, the weaver of palm leaves, and didn't concern me at all. It was just blind chance that had made me their recipient rather than anyone else.

My memories, or his? It doesn't matter. I mean, it's no longer important now. It was vital in the past, then it became clear to me that it was the content of the memories that was the most important thing, regardless of whether they belonged to me or to someone else.

Yes, there are things that are important in themselves, regardless of anything else.

Through his memories that poured out in my head, or my memories retrieved from a distant time, if you like, I learned of the crime of murder and the episode of betrayal. I learned of repeated dreams that turned Yazid ibn Abihi's life into hell. With time, he was no longer able to distinguish between his dreams and his reality. He had become a prisoner in the grip of the interpreter of his dreams, Malik ibn 'Udayy the copyist. In his youth, he would resort to his imam and his sheikh, al-Hasan al-Basri, to interpret his visions, and he continued in this way even after he had embraced the teachings of Wasil ibn 'Ata' on the denial of fate. With the death of al-Basri, dreams more like nightmares became more frequent, and there was no alternative but to look for another interpreter. He knew that al-Basri had no substitute and no one that could rival him in knowledge, but despite that he fell into the clutches of the copyist with no resistance. Not from stupidity or oversight on his part, but because of the sound judgment and cunning of the man. He seemed to know his secrets even before he had told him of his dreams. He was skilled in language, able to play with words with ease, and my old friend was weak when confronted with masters of language.

Malik the copyist had been a pupil of al-Hasan al-Basri in his youth and had befriended the Mu'tazilites for some time. Like Yazid, he proclaimed his allegiance to the doctrine of Wasil ibn 'Ata' al-Ghazzal, and his beliefs relating to the "position between the two positions" and the rejection of fate. But he subsequently rebelled against him. It was said that he had become a heretic or reverted to Mandeism or Manichaeism, his first faith.

No one can say with certainty what happened to him. All these assertions spread later, after he had wandered aimlessly in the lanes and alleys of Basra, sitting for hours in the Mirbad or forgetting himself as he stared at the boats crossing the marshes loaded with people and goods. He was sometimes out of sight for days. No one knew where he had hidden himself and no one cared if he appeared again. Meanwhile, he would sit like someone taken by surprise beside a jasmine shrub that was almost hidden among the vineyards and palm groves—a jasmine shrub that used to drop its flowers in greater numbers than similar plants. He would gaze at the flowers that had fallen to the grass, not speaking or moving, as if waiting for the dead jasmine to bring him a message from the bowels of the earth, but the humble earth preferred to bury its messages in its depths.

At first, the copyist enjoyed nothing but complete respect, then the respect turned into pity, and in time the pity turned into annoyance and mockery because of his strange ways and habits, until he disappeared for two years and returned rich, with all the signs of piety and reverence, distributing many gifts and presents. So people forgot his strange ways they had seen before.

As these details shine in my head, many memories of my more recent life as Hisham Khattab disappear behind them—with the exception of memories linked to that long-lost world, like everything to do with that girl who looked like she had just stepped out of a painting by Marc Chagall when I saw her for the first time. Even though I could not put my finger on the point of resemblance, I thought she looked like Bella Rosenfeld. I was fascinated at this time by Bella, and something in the girl's spirit and outlook reminded me of her as she appeared in her painted version. But how disappointed I was when the stupid girl started to imitate Bella's appearance.

To start with, she dyed her hair black and cut it short in the carré style, exactly like Bella in the picture I gave her. I could accept this, but what made it too much for me to bear was that she started wearing funny, almost ludicrous clothes, perhaps out of a desire to imitate Chagall's wife and inspiration. Imagine a young woman living at the beginning of the twenty-first century wearing clothes belonging to the first quarter of the twentieth century!

During that period, I also noticed how eager she was to blend in with others and live outside herself. She would go to the screenings at the Cultural Cinema Center in Sharif Street every week, and she was particularly fond of French cinema. We would come out of a film and head for the Zahrat al-Bustan, or the Hurriyya, or the Hamidiyya Market café, and we would immerse ourselves in conversation. I observed that she would take with her the facial expressions and gestures of the actresses in the film we'd just seen: Catherine Deneuve, Jean Seberg, Anna Karina, or Jane Birkin.

Then I realized that she did not stop with actresses, but often copied the movements and gestures of ordinary people: a friend of hers who bumped into us in the street, or someone she had just met, like a waitress in a café or a shop assistant. But what I couldn't bear was the way she repeated some of my own facial expressions and eccentricities of speech; it was as if I was in front of a mirror that reflected my image after a few seconds or gazing at a parrot that liked to be my echo.

She did this subtly, perhaps without realizing what she was doing, with just a look, a raised eyebrow, picking at her nose, or playing with her hair, inclining her head at a certain angle like one actress or another, shutting her eyes while laughing, or rubbing her chin to indicate her nervousness like I do. For good or ill, my eyes picked up on the quietist and subtlest of gestures. I don't say this out of pride, for this ability represented a punishment, not a blessing to me.

I met her once by chance, and this was the last meeting between us. She had come back to put on her own clothes— not those she believed were close to Bella Rosenfeld's style. Most likely, she hadn't been copying anyone's movements. But how would I know? Perhaps she was imitating the gestures of someone I didn't know. She started to talk mechanically, and I guessed she was disappointed because I hadn't told her I was coming to Cairo that day. I didn't make any excuses, even to mollify her. I said to myself that I didn't owe her or anyone else any excuse or explanation. Despite that, at the bottom of my heart I felt I owed her some recognition, for she rather than anyone else had shown me the beginning of the thread without knowing it. Ever since I had taken her copy of the *Great Interpretation of Dreams* attributed to the Imam Muhammad Ibn Sirin from her hands, my life had begun to change, and I had become more connected with the past.

I saw the title of the book and the name of Ibn Sirin on the cover, but they didn't pass peacefully as they had done in the past. A memory bell rang in my head, quiet and apprehensive at first, before turning into a constant resounding thump.

I opened the volume, thumbed through it quickly, and by chance happened on the name of Imam al-Din al-Hasan al-Basri. I continued thumbing through and my eye fell on a sight familiar to me from a long time ago, of angels plucking jasmine from the orchards of Basra. After that, jasmine occupied my dreams again and began to show me the depths of my soul. Nothing happens in this world by chance. Everything happens for the sake of something else. Every event, no matter how small, is the key to opening a particular box; all we have to do is to take note and register which box the key fits.

Even if we become confused and insert the wrong keys, so that not a single box or door opens to us, we can be certain that this is not by chance but is happening for some specific purpose—an important purpose, even if our limited understanding cannot grasp its dimensions.

For myself, I found my most important key (I will not say *all* my keys), which helped me to open the box of the past, buried under a jasmine bush at the edge of a vineyard in the city of language, imams, and jasmine.

While I was standing in front of the window, looking at the bombax tree with its orange flowers, I started to recall the face of a girl in which I had seen the image of Bella Rosenfeld. A girl who was a mirror, reflecting the expressions and gestures of people in front of her. Afterward, I wondered why I had not tolerated this trait of hers. Then I thought again and recalled that I seldom tolerated other people's faults or errors that affected me. I might forget or ignore them for a while, but I never really tolerated them. Toleration is overrated; it is barren and foolish. If the tired soul of Yazid ibn Abih had tolerated what had happened to him, I wouldn't now be preoccupied with him, wanting to take revenge for him, murdered by not knowing who I should direct my desire for vengeance against.

Perhaps because of all this, no previous emotional relationship of mine had lasted more than a few months, and some had ended even before they had begun. I sometimes felt I was searching with a magnifying glass for defects in any girl in front of me and making myself feel dissatisfied with this one or that one too easily, but I quickly thrust this feeling aside and tried to convince myself that some people had been created to live on their own with no companion or friend; they had been born loaded with an overwhelming anger and resentment that they didn't know how to direct, and if it happened that life compelled them to take a companion on whom they could rely in their times of weakness, they would deal with him, deep down, as if he and the void were equals.

I wonder now if Malik ibn 'Udayy the copyist and his betrayal of Yazid ibn Abih was not the cause of my predicament, and I wonder if Mujiba, a woman I never met or knew in my present life, was the reason I was cautious of women. Was that line of Amal Dunqul's, "A kick from a horse, which left a wound on my forehead and taught the heart to take care," relevant to me?

When I was first getting to know Mervat, or the Bella Rosenfeld of the age, I behaved like a naive lover. I would stay awake, totally preoccupied with her. Her image would appear to me as I ate or read or argued with my beloved heretic, and my thoughts would become confused.

I loved French films because of her; I read about Godard and Truffaut, among others, and I loved Jane Birkin, Anna

Karina, Jeanne Moreau and the rest just because I loved Mervat, there was no other reason. But something was making me tense and uneasy. In real life, she seemed to me to be gentle and calm, but in my dreams she was different. I often felt uncomfortable in dreams that brought us together.

I exploited her passion for *The Great Interpretation of Dreams,* attributed to the Imam Muhammad Ibn Sirin, and started to ask her to interpret my dreams. At the next meeting, she brought the book with her and showed me Ibn Sirin's interpretation of the symbols that had appeared to me.

I remember one dream in particular in which I had first seen myself in a ship in the middle of a sea before fleeing from the ship to a massive mountain. She produced an explanation from the volume of Ibn Sirin that implied ruin and destruction, because my dream alluded to the story of the son of Noah, when he refused to embark on his father's ark, thinking that the mountain would keep him safe from the flood.

She was gloomy and frowned as she explained this to me, but I tried to cheer her by making fun of myself and my dreams. I didn't tell her that she had appeared to me on top of the mountain, and for that reason I had left the boat to join her.

At that time, she had not yet started to imitate the gestures of other women. I would borrow Ibn Sirin's book from her, even though I had an old copy of it. Every time I read her copy, my heart would quiver in my chest, and I would feel an agitation mingled with fear and caution, followed inexplicably by a headache. Time and again I would go back to that dream, which the Imam al-Hasan al-Basri had interpreted to mean the departure of the Basran ulema. It awakened something hidden deep inside me, a feeling that he belonged to me and I to him, and that I was estranged from everything that surrounded me in my present life.

But the image only became entirely clear to me when the heretic surprised me one day with a rare work that he had in his possession. Of course, he only did this after he had put a copy of the Qur'an on the table between us and asked me to swear not to reveal the secret of the work unless he had given me permission. He then told me that he intended to edit and publish it later, and that its greatest importance lay in the fact that it told the story of the lives and everyday concerns of ordinary people in an age whose works were dominated by a concern with the lives of the eminent. He didn't tell me that I would find a lot in the book about Yazid ibn Abihi, whom I had asked him about previously. He left me to find this out by myself. I didn't press him on why he hadn't set my mind at rest with an answer that would sate my thirst for information when I asked him the first time. I knew him well enough not to put that sort of question to him.

I gathered from him that the author Malik ibn 'Udayy the copyist was completely unknown; there was no mention of him in any of the writings relating to this period, though what he had written in his book had shown that he was a contemporary of the Imam al-Hasan al-Basri, Ibn Sirin, Wasil ibn 'Ata', and 'Amr ibn 'Ubayd al-Bab, had witnessed the rise of the Mu'tazilite school in Basra, and had lived for almost a hundred years.

The heretic didn't let me borrow the book, but he let me read it in the private sitting room in his apartment.

He would shut the door behind him and leave me there for hours. From time to time, he would bring a plate of fruit, a cup of coffee, or a glass of tea, then immediately leave to go about his own business. Once, I discovered that the door that opened onto the staircase had been closed on me from the outside. This didn't surprise me, for despite his trust in me, he couldn't completely rid himself of his caution and suspicions. Otherwise, he would not have been the person I came to know so well.

I memorized particular sections of the book so I knew them by heart, then copied other sections—the ones in which the copyist, or the interpreter of dreams, as he was called, talked about his companion Yazid ibn Abihi and the stages of his relationship with him, and then about the relationship of the copyist with Mujiba, Yazid's wife.

I felt enormous grief when my master's apartment was burned, with all his books and treasures, together with him and his wife and daughter. I was sad for them, of course, but my greatest sorrow was for the rare books and volumes that had been reduced to ashes, and especially the work that had opened a door for me to know what had previously been kept secret for centuries. I had gotten to know myself in Yazid. Not everything the copyist mentioned in his confessional book agreed with what I subsequently recalled about the same events, but he had at least been the spur that helped me to capture and repossess that old memory. And he had allowed me to find out part of what had followed the betrayal of Yazid.

The inquiry into the fire in my master's apartment attributed the blaze to an electrical short circuit. The investigators ignored some neighbors' statements about cries for help from the apartment before the fire, and that the fire crews had ignored the neighbors' repeated communications, despite promising each time that a fire engine would come immediately to the stated address.

In the days afterward, I rearranged some passages that I had copied, added some other parts that I had memorized, and supplemented these with certain other events mentioned in the book that I could recall. I was trying to reconstruct the overall sequence of the story of Yazid, the copyist, and Mujiba, as narrated by the copyist himself, who included in it some of the writings of the palm weaver.

I wanted it for myself, as I realized that it would help me, over a shorter or longer period, to recall all the details of that old life I had forgotten. I didn't think of publishing it, or of referring directly or indirectly to Malik's book, not because I had promised my master not to reveal his secret without his permission—for promises like this are of no importance when the matter is concerned with knowledge—but rather on the basis that no one would believe me. And even if someone happened to believe me, they would probably not be interested in something written by someone completely unknown, whose work could not be edited after the only available copy had been lost.

2

From a window that is not, and could never be, my own, I gaze at some bright orange flowers and think of fire, of its power and vigor, and I realize that it can swallow almost anything. But there are some things that fire cannot consume, things that remain with us and come to an end only if we ourselves are burned.

Fire can do nothing with memory, for example. Memory is extinguished only from within, consuming itself and conspiring with forgetfulness against itself if it chooses and wishes to disappear and fade away, exactly like a torch that slowly fades if it doesn't find air and fuel to keep it alight.

Memory is the sister and companion of fire, but it is a cold, humble sister that does not want to attract attention to its power and what it can do. It is the shadow of fire, if you like.

That is what I know now. I believe that it is more powerful even than fire, for the latter can consume a man and his wife and daughter so that they become dust with no way of telling its origin; it can turn an apartment of four rooms and a hall into a ruined area covered by dust and soot; it can destroy a rich library, and its pleasure in consuming a rare work is greater than its pleasure in consuming anything else. As for memory, it can reconstruct all this, if it wants to, in the imagination; it can revive it and prevent attempts to hide it and muddle it. In my imagination, my master was moving; he talked and walked and created a clamor that was more than I could bear. His wife and daughter were in black clothes, which did not reveal their identities, strutting about inside me, gossiping together, each carrying a tray with a cup of coffee on it, knocking on a door leading to a sitting room with another door leading to the outside staircase. I sit with the father in the room, pretending to listen to him, while my mind is preoccupied with other plans, which do not include him.

There is a rare work in my mind as well, whose lines I devour greedily, and which I almost know by heart from so much repetition. A work which I could almost have written, though I am not the author. A work that talks about me, about an old self who resembles me. It reveals it and strips it bare in front of me. It strips me bare in front of myself, although the author meant to expose himself and lay bare his own faults in the hope of atoning for them.

I burned the book and the library and the house, with all those in it, and fled the city. I deserted Bella and returned to al-Minya to live with my mother. Even so, the people I betrayed remained alive in my imagination. I do not feel regret, and have no sense of guilt. I am merely annoyed that the fire revealed its limitations in confronting memory.

How could I feed my memories to the fire? How could I escape them and save myself from their burden? No one discovered what I had done. I got away with it. The case was quickly closed. A short circuit. A common cause of fires that does not arouse suspicion. Anyone who said they heard shouting from my master's house before the fire was not taken seriously, and the fire destroyed any possible evidence.

It was a short circuit, certainly. Absolutely certainly. A perfect crime without a motive when assessed using conventional logic. I did not take a box of jewels from my master's house. I did not take any of the money or rare books or valuable manuscripts contained within the library. And even if I had, there was no way to prove it.

I pledged everything to destruction, but it still would not perish. It remained alive inside me. My master and his daughter and wife. The sitting room in all its detail, the book with its letters and the secrets it revealed: they were not to be exposed to the public like that, even if no one knew anything about the people it referred to.

A week before the fire, my beloved heretic told me he wanted to publish the book with a detailed introduction. It was a rare piece of literature that he didn't want to keep to himself. He mentioned something about the unique style and powerful structure, and how the author avoided all exaggerated linguistic elaborations. He asked me if I agreed with him that this work by Malik the copyist differed from everything else written in its time. I agreed that it did, for he was right from an artistic point of view, though deep n down I was concerned with other aspects, for the book had shed light on the dark places of my memory and reminded me of what was hidden under layer upon layer of ignorance and forgetfulness.

I was interested in the case of Yazid ibn Abihi—my own case, if you like. I don't know why he was so eager to record everything that happened to him. Did he want to cleanse himself through writing? Did he want to confess to the pages and manuscripts? What was this stupidity, Yazid? But you weren't the only one who wanted to cleanse himself. Malik ibn 'Udayy the copyist was your companion in that as well. He recorded the details of his double betrayal of you, then filled out his work with what you had written earlier, recounting how he had ransacked your old house in a search for your bundles of manuscripts after Mujiba had told him she had read some of what you were writing.

How I wish I hadn't asked the heretic about you at the beginning! If only I had remained ignorant of the existence of this work by Malik the copyist. The heretic looked at me for a long time as he spoke of his intention to publish the book in his possession. I was unable to plumb his depths, and I was annoyed that he seemed beyond my understanding.

I encouraged him, of course, and proposed that I should help him in anything he thought appropriate. He thanked me and moved onto something else. He asked me to bring him some old manuscripts from a merchant who lived in Bab al-Shi'riyya, saying the man would wait for me at nine the following morning. He had started treating me as if I was just a private postman. No longer did he ask me, as he had in the past, about the most convenient times for me to go on this or that errand.

I didn't object, just as I didn't object when he started to include my thoughts and observations in his latest books and essays without attributing them to me. Who am I, anyway, that a prominent intellectual like him should attribute an opinion or idea to me?

I was embarrassed every time I found my ideas included in his writings, as though somehow I was the one in the wrong, as if I should hide for a while so that my master would not feel embarrassed if we happened to meet immediately afterward.

But my master never showed any sign of embarrassment. Sometimes I would offer a contrary opinion in the course of a heated argument, then a few minutes later I would find him adopting my opinion as if it was his own and he was trying to convince me of it. Sometimes I doubted myself, thinking that perhaps I hadn't actually said this a few minutes ago, my master had; something had confused me into thinking it was my own opinion.

In such a situation, I would nod my head in agreement, as if finally persuaded of what he was saying, and he would look contented and move the conversation onto another topic.

After the apartment had been destroyed by fire, with everyone and everything in it, and the cause of the incident attributed to a short circuit, I no longer felt that there was a place for me in Cairo, and I decided to go back to al-Minya and settle there as soon as possible.

We had already confirmed the death of my father in exile in Libya and established that he had died on his way from Libya to Kairouan in Tunisia. My mother's ailments included diabetes, with a fear of complications, and an intense, repeated abdominal pain caused by a stone in the right kidney that needed to be passed. I left everything that was behind me and in front of me and went back to be beside her. I found it a suitable opportunity to move all my activities there and content myself with periodic visits to Cairo to keep up with the dealers in old books and their customers. It also suited me to turn the page with Bella, and to put some hundreds of kilometers between us.

3

Jasmine in my head, jasmine in my guts and bowels, jasmine filling the world around me. I choke on it, I gag on the smell of it, I yearn for a world devoid of it and its smell. It is no longer just my dreams that are drowning in this harsh white flower, which has left the land of my sleep and moved to the geography of my waking. It has conquered everything around me. I don't see it in blossom on its bushes, but fallen, piled up in the lanes and alleys or flying in the air during a storm. The other smells abate, my mother's mint and basil vanish, everything else disappears, and I alone remain to confront piles of dead flowers, whose smell turns my sensitive chest to a raging furnace that burns me from the inside.

I cough nonstop, and my muscles are ripped apart one after the other. I close my eyes, wishing there was a way for me to suspend my senses of smell and hearing, but the smell becomes thicker. I open my eyes and find myself walking amid wide palm groves and vineyards. I see no jasmine, but the smell and the thought of it cling to me. With the eyes of my imagination, I can see rows of shrubs, with transparent angels bending over them to pluck their flowers. The flowers leave the angels and soar toward the sky. They sparkle, and their whiteness is almost dazzling. As I stare at them, faces appear, which turn into bodies. I reply in a voice that has no connection with my own voice, as I know it: This is my sheikh, al-Hasan al-Basri; this is my imam, Wasil ibn 'Ata'; this is 'Amr ibn 'Ubayd al-Bab, and that man busily recording is Malik the copyist. I see myself among them, sometimes running behind al-Basri and at other times turning toward Abu Hudhayfa. I figure that I am torn between the two. No, I am the one to arbitrate between them. But how can a weak person like me judge between them, when they are who they are? I put the idea out of my mind as I carry on walking, my eyes trained upward to where the flowers are, and the imams ascend in a night journey whose dimensions I cannot fathom.

I arrive at a vineyard collapsing into its trellises and feel it is my homeland, my resting place. Nearby, I catch sight of the marshes, as if I had lived my whole life there. I sit on the ground, gazing at the dried-out vines, then turn to stare at a murky horizon, and my heart pains me.

Suddenly, it occurs to me that my journey ends here. I think of digging up the ground, but I cannot find a spade, so I give up on the idea. I lie down on my back, dreaming that the grass under me is turning green and that the vine is returning to its former state. Surely it must have flourished and blossomed at some time. In some obscure way, I know that it dried up from sorrow and depression, overcome by death on the day my old self was buried in the depths of the graveyard. After decomposing, my body was not fit to give it life. It was a treacly medicine, but when its dose increased, it became a poison with no antidote. This improvised grave of mine was dug and left wide open to the sky for a little, so the balance of its surroundings was disturbed. I was murdered and buried with no ablution or funeral prayer, and my murderer planted a jasmine bush over my grave, which grew and branched and conspired with him to hide his crime. No one asked what had brought the jasmine to the edge of a leafy vineyard. I know this jasmine. It stretched its branches, climbing in all directions, and they penetrated the vineyard, intruding on it and invading its trellises. From my hiding place deep underground, I watched its white flowers, which spread in all directions throughout the vineyard. I imagined angels descending from heaven every night to pluck the jasmine, and I imagined Basra with no jasmine and no orchards. Was my sheikh and imam wrong? Was he wrong in his interpretation of my vision? I don't think so. After my dream, despite the fact that the scholars of my city had actually passed away, it escaped him that the vision also concerned me, and also the jasmine, my jasmine that nourished itself on my body.

The woman who lives with me and violates the privacy of my room twice daily, once in the morning and again in the evening, says that there are no orchards nearby, and that the little garden overlooked by my window has no jasmine in it, not even the type of jasmine known as *full*, just a single palm tree and some bombax trees with their orange flowers—like that tree where she found me asleep on a marble chair set underneath it one morning. She was angry when I woke up, her eyes flashing with a frightening look, while behind her stood the doorman, breathing noisily as if he had just stopped running. She asked me how I had tricked her as I slipped out of my room and accused me of deliberately disturbing her. She sighed impatiently when I told her I had eaten the moon and caused the world to grow dark, and that I was surrounded by the smell of jasmine when I woke, and when I could find no jasmine awake, I went back to sleep again.

She is not convinced by my protests and takes no notice of what I tell her. She only listens to me with a puzzled look, which reminds me of all the riddles I have been unable to solve and that continue to whisper to me that layers upon layers of ambiguity are spread over my world.

She calls me Hisham. I tell her I am Yazid ibn Abih, who was assassinated and buried in a hole on the edge of a vineyard near the Shatt al-'Arab. She shakes her head impatiently then calls me Hisham again. I do not reply.

Sometimes I feel sorry for her; she is not to blame for any of this. Perhaps she secretly curses the day she got to know me after I had returned from al-Minya to finally live in Cairo. She didn't understand what a mess she had got herself into when she joined her life to mine. She hardly knew anything about my past and wanted to fill the chasm of her ignorance in unending questions, some of which I could understand the purpose of, while others remained opaque. I would answer her mechanically, but she would ignore the suppressed tone of annoyance in my voice and continue her irritating questions.

She asked for the source of the song with which my mother used to lament her lost youth, and I would reply that I had no mothers. She would correct herself by changing "mother" into "the woman who thinks she is my mother," and eagerly await my reply.

I would reply half-consciously, and she would ask for the details of a long-past day when the traffic had been stopped because some official's motorcade was passing. I told her I hardly remembered that day, and she would try to jog my memory. I would interrupt her to talk to her about al-Hasan al-Basri, Wasil ibn 'Ata', and the city of language, imams and orchards. Then her voice would grow angry as she asked me to look around and recognize the details of my reality.

Assailed again by the smell of jasmine, I would grow irritated with her and move toward the window. I would look at the small garden, paved except for some small areas that had been left for the cultivation of flowers and bonsai trees. My gaze would pass over them to look farther away, where I could see mango trees weighed down with fruit, partially visible portions of a school playground and part of a soccer field. I could sense the woman fiddling with the edges of her house dress as she prepared to leave. When she shut the door behind her, I did not turn around. I knew she would be back in the morning, even though I wished she wouldn't.

Hardly anyone else comes into my room. I hear faint whispers outside. From time to time a hysterical scream rings out, and the sound of footsteps reaches me from the corridor linking the rooms, but except for the woman who leaves a tray of food at the door for me three times a day and comes to speak to me once in the morning and again in the evening, I hardly see anyone, except during the few hours I spend crouching in the garden, spying on a few scattered pedestrians passing by through a chink in the wall. There's a stifled noise in the villa that my ears cannot distinguish; only my soul is aware of it as it picks up the signs of hidden tension. More than once in a single night I am woken by a clatter in the room above me, as if someone is disturbing the night's quiet by moving a heavy table or chair. I go back to sleep, only to be awakened again by a constant banging emanating from the same source. The person who lives above me never stops stamping around, moving the furniture here and there and banging across the wooden floor with heavy footsteps.

He seems to be sending me a message. I shake off the idea—it seems too stupid—and surrender to sleeplessness. He doesn't sleep either, for the hubbub from his room hardly stops. I pity him his situation, but I feel no guilt over not suffering with him. I have enough of my own to cope with.

It occurs to me to complain to my constant companion about the noise at night, then I decide not to do so when I imagine how her eyes will flash when I speak to her, even if just to complain. She will think it is my response to her annoying me. When I complained the last time, she denied the existence of any noise. Her eyes grew wider as she told me, glowering, that the villa consisted of just two stories and that a third storey did not exist, before adding that no one lived in it except us.

Sometimes when she calls me Hisham, I don't bother to

correct my name, and she seems pleased that I've accepted what she said and reverted to the identity that satisfies her. It is useless to explain to her that I am Hisham as much as I am Yazid, but that my identity as Hisham is clearly recognized and doesn't need defending like my identity as Yazid ibn Abihi.

Should I tell her the story of the Bedouin woman who, when asked who was her favorite son, replied, "The youngest, until he grows up; the sick one, until he gets better, and the absent one until he returns"?

In the same way, Yazid is my favorite identity, and the one closest to me, because he is the one who needs my sympathy and support, he was the betrayed one whose spirit hovers above me wherever I go. The smell of jasmine surrounds me just as it surrounded his grave, after his murderer had planted the tree above it. How can I flee from this deathly jasmine when its smell will not leave me?

She will not understand me if I explain all this to her. She will be content to lament her fate that threw her together with me. She says I seemed perfect when we first met, so much so that she praised God and thanked him for his goodness and for her good fortune. None of this concerns me, what concerns me now is that she should let me escape from the noise of the person living on the upper floor.

I asked her about him once, and I trust her description of him as a disturbing case. For her, people are just cases, some disturbing and others not. She takes no notice, it seems, of the fact that some people are a bundle of naked nerves exposed to constant conflagration. When I confronted her with this opinion of mine, she denied describing him as a disturbing case. She said, "How should I describe someone who doesn't exist?" And she asked me to stop making things up.

Despite this, I sometimes find myself revealing things to her that I never imagined I would tell a soul. Something about her induces other people to tell her their innermost secrets—or perhaps it's that injection of tranquillizers that she plants in my arm from time to time that brings about these sudden bouts of revelation.

I'm not sure, but her injection makes me calm and compliant and quiets the devils in my head for a time. For a little while, it makes me forget everything to do with Yazid and whets my appetite to talk and discuss things. Its contents flow through my veins, so I am hardly aware of the woman sitting in the room with me. She turns into a recording machine or just a pair of ears into which I pour whatever is bothering me or weighing heavily upon me.

I ask her about my mother, and why she doesn't come to visit us here. She replies with a question: Didn't you tell me you had no mothers?

I ignore her sharp wit and repeat the question. She looks away and changes the subject to avoid answering.

I long for our apartment in al-Minya and wish I could resume sleeping in my familiar bed. I resolve not to moan about my mother's constant raving or her nonstop complaining.

The last time we were together was just before I moved to Cairo. We were walking with each other beside the Nile when she tripped, and afterward she fell into a deep sleep from which I was unable to awaken her. After I shook her several times without success, I wondered whether she was still in the same coma. I would like to go back to the al-Minya apartment to check on her. She certainly must have grown tired of the Nile and gone back to water her pots of mint and basil and cook her delicious food. I will tell her what is bothering me, and perhaps she will finally understand what has kept me from her all these years, what has set a gulf between us that it is hard to bridge.

In our last year together, her mind was constantly wandering. She would tell me about her mother and brother and her grandmother, that woman who loved to wander the lanes that led to the neighboring villages, as if looking for something lost before the beginning of time. She also talked about her father, the merchant who loved Layla Murad so much that he named his own daughter Layla and his son Murad. She often told me of her brother Murad. She said she loved him more than anyone else in the world and cried when she remembered how kind he was to her and the way he looked after her.

I tell my companion, who looks nothing like Bella, that I want to go back to al-Minya to look after my mother, and she replies that that would be impossible. She asks after my master and the last time I saw him and asks me to let her hear the sermon of Wasil ibn 'Ata' from memory.

"If you know it by heart, as you claim," she added, and my hatred for her increased.

I turned my back on her and spoke with my eyes closed.

"Praise be to God, the eternal, the everlasting, from the beginning of creation to its end, sublime in his profundity and profound in his sublimity. Time does not encompass him, nor can place contain him. He is not burdened with remembering what he has created; he did not create it to an existing pattern but brought it into being anew, and set it in order; so he made well everything he created, and perfected his will; made clear his wisdom and demonstrated his divinity. So, praise to Him, whose judgment cannot be amended, and whose authority cannot be resisted. Everything is subservient to his might, everything bows to his authority. His goodness encompasses everything. Not a single grain escapes him, he is the all-hearing, all-knowing ..."

Then my memory grew cloudy, the words became a jumble, and then they faded, one by one. I felt faint, as though swarms of ants were eating my brain, pricking it gently at first, then quickly harder. I collapsed on the bed nearby, unable to look in her direction. She lifted her head at last from her papers, came up to me, and lifted the cuff of my shirt as she prepared a syringe and planted it in the vein. Through the mist I could see my hand pushing my mother, worn out by illness and old age, toward the water. Then I was standing following a funeral, and everyone was consoling and encouraging me. After that, I heard the confused voice of the heretic asking me what rare book I was speaking about. I told him the book of Malik the copyist, and he looked at me as if I were a madman. I retrieved the situation and told him that I was confused and exhausted, and in need of rest. I left promising to return soon, and he followed me with knitted eyebrows and other signs of preoccupation apparent on his face.

The mist thickens further and becomes a dark curtain

separating me from everything else. My body goes limp—no, the whole world goes limp. It is no longer aware of me, and I in my turn am no longer aware of it. I feel that I am in a hole, covered with layers of earth, amid a pitch-black darkness, punctuated by the fragrance of jasmine that allows no sleep.

Shanghai, October 2018

LIST OF HISTORICAL FIGURES, PLACE NAMES, AND OTHER TERMS

Note: *Mansoura Ez-Eldin's* The Orchards of Basra *not only brings together the worlds of contemporary Egypt and medieval Baghdad, but also mingles historical characters with fictional ones. This short list provides basic information about the main historical characters, geographical place names, and some other terms included in the work.*

'Abbasiyya. District in central Cairo, where Saint Mark's Coptic Orthodox Cathedral and the medical faculty of Ain Shams University are located.

'Abdallah ibn 'Umar ibn 'Abd al-'Aziz, 700s–c.750. Umayyad prince, briefly governor of Iraq in 744–745.

Abu Bakr al-Nazzam, 775/782–836/845. Mu'tazilite theologian and poet, born in Basra.

Abu Hayyan al-Tawhidi, 923–1023. Intellectual and philosopher who worked as a scribe in various cities in the Islamic world.

'Amr ibn 'Ubayd al-Bab, d. 761. A student of the early theologian al-Hasan Al-Basri, and one of the earliest leaders of the Mu'tazilite movement.

al-Azhar. Mosque and university founded in Cairo in AD 970, which remains the leading institution in the Islamic world for the study of Sunni theology.

Bani Mazar. Rural town in Egypt, located in the Minya Governorate, on the west bank of the Nile.

Banu Hilal. A confederation of Arab tribes from the Najd region of the Arabian Peninsula who emigrated across North Africa in the 11th century. Their journeyings formed the basis for an extended epic poem known as the *Sirat Bani Hilal*, which was widely performed throughout the Arab world until recently.

Bashshar ibn Burd, 714–783. Influential poet of Persian ancestry, blind from birth, who grew up in Basra.

Basra. City in southern Iraq, of which it is the main port, founded in AD 636.

Ezbekiyya. District in central Cairo, once renowned for its gardens and Opera House (burned down in 1971), and a site for second-hand booksellers and other traders.

Farid al-Din al-'Attar, c. 1145 – c. 1221, Persian Sufi (mystical) poet, best known for his work *The Conference of the Birds*.

al-Hajjaj ibn Yusuf al-Thafaqi, 661–714. Administrator during the Umayyad caliphate, who served as governor of Iraq (694–714).

al-Hasan al-Basri, 642–728. Early Muslim theologian, whose name is often associated with abstinence and poverty, and with the early development of Sufism (Islamic mysticism).

Heliopolis. Residential suburb of Cairo, located to the north-east of the city, close to the airport and Madinat al-Nasr.

Ibadis. Branch of Islam which emerged about 60 years after the death of the Prophet Muhammad in AD 632.

Ibn al-Rawandi, 827–911. Mu'tazilite scholar who later rejected the doctrines of the Mu'tazilis.

Ikhwan al-Safa' ("Brethren of Purity"). A secret society of Muslim philosophers, active in Basra in the 9th and 10th centuries, whose doctrines were based on Neo-Platonism.

al-Jahiz, 776–868/869. Arab author and polymath, born in Basra, sometimes known as "the father of Arabic prose."

Kairouan. City in Tunisia, founded around 670, which became an important center for Islamic scholarship.

al-Karkh. The western part of Baghdad.

Khalid ibn Safwan. Orator at the Umayyad and Abbasid courts.

al-Khalil ibn Ahmad al-Farahidi, 718–786 or 791. Arab philologist, lexicographer and leading grammarian of Basra, who compiled the first extant dictionary of the Arabic language.

Korba. A district of Heliopolis, a suburb to the north of Cairo.

Kufa. City in southern Iraq, about 100 miles south of Baghdad, founded in 638 and an important pilgrimage site for Shi'ite Muslims.

Madinat Nasr [Victory City]. Modern residential suburb on the east side of Cairo dating from the late1950s.

al-Mansour, c. 714–775. The second Abbasid caliph, who founded the city Madinat as-Salam ("city of peace") which became the core of the Imperial capital Baghdad.

al-manzila bayn al-manzilatayn ("the intermediate position"). Doctrine developed by Wasil ibn 'Ata' to describe the status of a Muslim who has committed a major sin.

Midian. Geographical region in the northwest of the Arabian Peninsula mentioned in the Tanakh and Qur'an.

al-Minya. City in Upper Egypt, located on the Nile about 100 miles south of Cairo.

Mirbad. Marketplace on the edge of the southern Iraqi city of Basra which served as a meeting-place for poets and intellectuals.

Muhammad ibn Sirin, 654–728. Early Islamic writer, born in Basra and author of the *Great Interpretation of Dreams*.

Murji'a. ("those who postpone"). Early Islamic sect, who argued that God alone has the right to judge whether or not a Muslim has become an apostate.

Mu'tazilites ("those who withdraw or stand apart"). Islamic school of theology (*kalām*) which flourished in Basra and Baghdad in the 8th to 10th centuries and whose proponents were variously regarded as either heretics or freethinkers. The Mu'tazilites placed emphasis on the oneness of God (*tawhid*), on the status of the Qur'an as created rather than eternal, and on man's freewill.

Samawa. City in southern Iraq, located between Baghdad and Basra.

al-Sayyid Badawi, 1200–1276. Sufi mystic born in Fez, Morocco, who settled in Tanta, Egypt in 1236 and developed a posthumous reputation as a Muslim saint. His birth is celebrated annually in a popular festival known as a mawlid.

Sharqia. Egyptian governorate located north of Cairo.

Shatt al-'Arab. River about 120 miles in length at the confluence of the Euphrates and Tigris rivers in southern Iraq.

Shu'ayb. Ancient pre-Islamic prophet, mentioned in the Qur'an and traditionally identified with the biblical Jethro, Moses' father-in-law.

'Ukaz. Marketplace and site of fair and poetry contests in pre-Islamic Mecca, where warring tribes could meet and trade peaceably.

Wasil ibn 'Ata' [al-Ghazzal] c. 699-749. Muslim theologian, active in Basra, often considered to be the founder of the Mu'tazilite movement, and author of the doctrine of *al-manzila bayn al-manzilatayn*.

Zamalek. Prestigious district of Cairo, located on an island in the Nile River.

Ziyad ibn Abihi, c. 622–673. Statesman and administrator, who served as the governor of Basra in 665–670 and later as the first governor of Iraq

Zuhair ibn Abi Sulma, c. 520-c. 609. Pre-Islamic poet, author of one of the poems in the famous collection known as the *Mu'allaqat* ("Suspended poems").

ABOUT THE AUTHOR

Mansoura Ez-Eldin is an Egyptian novelist and short story writer, born in 1976. She is the author of six novels and three short story collections and her works have been translated into more than ten languages. In 2009 she was selected by the Beirut 39 Project as one of the best 39 Arab writers under the age of 40. In 2010, she was the youngest writer to be shortlisted for the International Prize for Arabic Fiction for her novel *Beyond Paradise*. *The Orchards of Basra* was longlisted for IPAF in 2021. Her work has been acknowledged by awards at Cairo Book Fair and Sharjah International Book Fair, as well as the Al-Multaqa Prize for the Arabic Short Story and the Sheikh Zayed Book Award. Her articles have been published in *The New York Times*, *Granta*, *A Public Space*, *Süddeutsche Zeitung* and *Neue Zürcher Zeitung* (NZZ). She currently works as the managing editor of the Egyptian weekly cultural magazine *Akhbar al-Adab* and is editor of its books section.

ABOUT THE TRANSLATOR

Paul G. Starkey has translated works by Adania Shibli, Mansoura Ez-Eldin, Youssef Rakha, Edwar al-Kharrat, Mahmoud Shukair, Jalal Barjas, and many others. He was Winner of the 2015 Saif Ghobash Banipal Prize for his translation of *The Book of the Sultan's Seal* (Interlink Books) by Youssef Rakha.